Stars will guide you *Home*

PRAISE FOR STUTI CHANGLE

'[Changle is known for her] relatable characters and inspiring message ... [her books make for] a popular read for those seeking guidance and inspiration on their own life journeys.'
—*The Economic Times*

'Stuti Changle wants to inspire youth to "make a move!"'
—*YourStory*

'Her book inspires you to listen to your heart and follow your inner calling!'
—*Dainik Bhaskar*

'Changle is known for her simple prose and memorable characters.'
—*Deccan Chronicle*

Stars will guide you *Home*

STUTI CHANGLE

HARPER FICTION

An Imprint of HarperCollins Publishers

First published in India by Harper Fiction 2025
An imprint of HarperCollins *Publishers*
HarperCollins *Publishers* India, Cyber City, Building 10-A,
Gurugram, Haryana – 122002, India
www.harpercollins.co.in

2 4 6 8 10 9 7 5 3 1

Copyright © Stuti Changle 2025

P-ISBN: 978-93-6989-065-1
E-ISBN: 978-93-6989-081-1

This is a work of fiction and all characters and incidents described in this book are the product of the author's imagination. Any resemblance to actual persons, living or dead, is entirely coincidental.

Stuti Changle asserts the moral right
to be identified as the author of this work.

All rights reserved. No part of this publication may be reproduced, stored in a retrieval system, or transmitted, in any form or by any means, electronic, mechanical, photocopying, recording or otherwise, without the prior permission of the publishers.

Without limiting the exclusive rights of any author, contributor or the publisher of this publication, any unauthorized use of this publication to train generative artificial intelligence (AI) technologies is expressly prohibited. HarperCollins also exercise their rights under Article 4(3) of the Digital Single Market Directive 2019/790 and expressly reserve this publication from the text and data-mining exception.

Typeset in 11/14 Sabon
by HarperCollins *Publishers* India Pvt. Ltd

Printed and bound at
Replika Press Pvt. Ltd.

This book is produced from independently certified FSC® paper to ensure responsible forest management.

HarperCollins *Publishers*, Macken House, 39/40 Mayor Street Upper, Dublin 1, D01 C9W8, Ireland

To those who have known loneliness, carried a broken heart, or felt lost along the way—may you always find your way back home, to yourself.

CONTENTS

My New Game	1
There Is No Magic	17
How Are You Today?	35
Bling and the Ring	40
The Delay	53
Why Are They a Perfect Match?	70
The City of Dreams	72
Home Away from Home	88
What Is Love?	105
First Love	109
Same but Different	117
Do I Know You?	134
Please Don't Break My Heart!	143
When Did It All Go Wrong?	159
I Will Find You	161

It Isn't Meant to Be	174
Whose Fault Was It?	189
Welcome Home!	191
Epilogue	203
Author's Note	211
Acknowledgements	213

'The world is our home. It is delusional to call your apartment home. Even worse to stick to the same place all through your life. If you've found love or happiness somewhere, you've found a home.'
— Ramy, *On the Open Road*

My New Game

Nirvaan

Friday, 9 December 2022
IIT Delhi, New Delhi

'You've got to have the will to build anything and everything from scratch in life.'

When does a person feel like they have achieved enough in life? We set goals for ourselves, and we achieve them. Then we set even bigger goals and march off on the quest to achieve them too. Sometimes, we're happy while on the journey and sometimes we wait desperately for the destination. But at no point do we ever feel fully satisfied with what we've accomplished.

But these goals that we're always chasing—are they even set by us? Or have they been imposed on us by society? Who is the master? Us or society? Has the modern world been designed as such? Are we like that circus-trained lion whose tricks are never enough for its master even though it risks its life to achieve them?

Then again, if we have nothing to chase, why would we even wake up every morning and live through the day? Won't it feel like death to be that purposeless?

I'm on the way to my alma mater, IIT Delhi, five years after having graduated as a computer science engineer. My mind has been flooded with existential thoughts since very early in the day, but let's shift our focus to the weather for a bit. If you've ever been to Delhi, you'll know how cold it gets during the winter. And if you've never been to the city, you would've definitely come across the *dilli-ki-sardi* memes on the internet. But this week hasn't been just plain cold; the weather has taken a magical turn, with heavy rain and chilly winds sweeping across the city. And that hasn't helped with how I'm feeling.

It seems like it was just yesterday when I was a student at IIT-D, and it's been hard to come to terms with the fact that in reality, many years have passed since then. I woke up in the morning today to a mixed bag of feelings in my heart. I was both happy and nervous all at once—happy because I was headed back to the campus after a long gap, despite living in the same city (although on an on-and-off basis); and nervous because I'm now an alum the students really look up to (I'm on the other side!). And to top it all, I'm also kind of sleepy because I wasted too much time on the internet last night, watching a new show on Netflix and then scrolling through the reels tab on Instagram.

When will I grow up?

'Ahh! I'm not a student anymore!' I sigh.

Rather, I'm on the panel of entrepreneurs who've been invited to the institute's very own Shark Tank-like pitching event called *Navachaar*, a forum run by and for IIT-D students and alumni. The word 'navachaar' roughly translates to innovation in English. I know this now because it's the first thing I googled while sitting on the toilet seat this morning. Now, my mother tongue is Malayalam, and I grew up in elite circles that value and propagate English like it's their very own language. My Hindi, therefore, is not very strong. I'm a victim here, and I really can't be blamed for this. But I'm making up for it in this new India that values our cultural roots like never before. I'm proud of my South Indian-accented English.

A little restless, I roll down the window of my car and partially stick my head out to breathe in the luxuriously fresh air that is rarer than *sanjeevani booti* in this polluted city. No, I'm not the one who's driving. Since I'm almost always on the go, I prefer to be driven by our driver, Veeru Uncle. He's been working for my family for so long now that he's one of us.

Anyway, I've been wanting to invest in a startup or an initiative that addresses this air pollution issue for a long time now. But I'm yet to either come up with an innovative idea myself or find a bunch of individuals interested in taking it up. Pity!

Raindrops tip-tap softly against the roof of the car, their rhythmic patter composing a soothing lullaby. The earthy aroma of wet soil that rises up when raindrops fall from the sky is pure magic. It wafts in through the open car window and makes my heart sing. It stirs up memories from my childhood, when we would make small paper boats and dance in muddy puddles after every rain. And then adulthood, especially in college, when the rains triggered that insane urge to smoke a cigarette and sip some hot ginger tea or coffee at a roadside stall, an urge so strong that it was like a gun held to your head by a gangster. You either do or die at a time like this.

Who says time machines aren't real? Because when we reach the campus a little later and drive past the entry gate, in the span of a single moment, I travel nine years back in time to when I first came to this place. So yeah, the gates of the institution are practically a time machine for me! The corroded pathways, the red brick towers, the central library—everything transports me to a time of my life that I miss the most. Some parts of the old buildings are hard to recognize now because they have been renovated, yet the feelings they evoke are the same. A rush of memories, some joyful and some not so great, flood my mind.

The rain has come down to a drizzle. I see students walking around and a few guys playing basketball. Their faces are unfamiliar and strange, but I feel a weird sense of belonging.

Nostalgia hugs me like a warm blanket on this cold, rainy morning, and I am reminded of the person I was when I first entered IIT-D. My mother had come to drop me in her fancy pink car. It was the first time I was going to be away from my family and live in a hostel with a bunch of crazy folks. And as it turned out, IIT-D's hostel life was exactly like the image I had in my mind after watching the famous film *3 Idiots*.

As my mother drove away after dropping me, I watched her car grow smaller and smaller until it vanished from sight. Tears rolled down my cheeks. This would be the second time in my life that I cried, but I never called my mother back nor did I ever mention this to her.

Incidentally, the first time I cried was just a few weeks before that, when Kiranjeet, the first love of my life, moved abroad to study at her uncle's dream university. She had no idea that I was there the day she left, looking at her from a distance as she said goodbye to her parents and disappeared into the vast entrance hall of the Indira Gandhi International Airport. Later, I sat in my best friend Vedant's car, parked on the road outside the airport, watching flights taking off and waving them goodbye. That was when I cried for the first time.

And that spot near the airport was, ironically, the same place where Kiranjeet and I had made out in the same car after our school farewell party. It was where I had felt both ecstatic and then devastated across a span of a few weeks. How was I to know when Kiranjeet and I were kissing and promising to meet each other more often that this very place was also going to mark the end of our relationship?

Because Kiranjeet had never loved me the way I loved her. She loved her ambitions more. I, on the other hand, had the opportunity to study at IIT Kanpur and pursue elective courses that were more suited to my interests, but I chose to stay back in Delhi only for her.

That night, I had sobbed helplessly on Vedant's shoulder as he drove me back home. Vedant is my dearest pal and only he knows that I'm capable of shedding tears—men are not supposed to cry after all! The rest of the world looks up to me as this motivational warrior on LinkedIn who's capable of taking over the universe with his intelligence and charm. I've been described as one of the most eligible and sought-after bachelors in the country by numerous magazines, but the truth is that I'm very lonely.

As we make our way towards the auditorium, we leave behind corners that echo with memories of late-night study sessions and youthful dreams. This place, my college, where I enrolled as a young boy with a broken heart, means so much to me. It was exactly the sort of place that I needed to be in to pave the way for the Nirvaan I've become now. My days here were a time of boundless possibilities, where every lecture sparked curiosity and every friendship felt eternal.

A bittersweet longing for those simpler days when I was filled with hopes and aspirations sweeps through me as nostalgia grips me harder. The person I've become now is stronger and more confident than ever. And this was exactly what I'd wanted for myself. I'm now a name to be reckoned with in the startup industry. I've made it in life, finally! I've arrived! I find myself filled with a sense of pride and gratitude.

Veeru Uncle drops me off at the main entrance of the auditorium building. The weathered facade of the red brick building stands tall and proud just like the old times. There are bougainvillea shrubs with magenta blooms dotting either side of the main entrance and vibrant green vines going all the way up to the top of the building. Each year, as new batches of students enrol at the institute, it's as if these creepers are filled with a renewed sense of vigour to grow. These vines are symbolic of the new life now, rising and falling with every passing year and breathing fresh energy into the timeless structure of this historic building.

'Namaste!' A beautiful young girl wearing a black business suit emerges out of nowhere, or so it seems.

'Hey, hi!' I say, snapping out of my thoughts.

'Hi, Nirvaan! We're thrilled to have you as one of the panellists today,' she chimes.

'Yes, I'm thrilled to be here too. I'm really looking forward to it. What's your name?' I find myself curious about her.

'I'm Shubha. It's my first semester here and I'm excited to be a volunteer at this event.'

'Nice to meet you, Shubha. Tell me, what made you volunteer for the event?' I ask.

'Well, I wanted to get involved with the extracurricular activities here on campus and meet new people as well. I also have an interest in exploring the world of entrepreneurship. I don't know if I want to start a company like you someday, but ...' she trails off.

I'm not at all surprised by her answer. She's simply following the script that every new student follows. In fact, I used to talk exactly like her when I was in my first semester.

'I also participated in such events when I was a student here. Now that I'm older, I always enjoy sharing my experiences and insights with young, aspiring entrepreneurs,' I say, wanting to build a rapport with her.

'Awesome! I'm really looking forward to hearing what you have to say during the panel discussion, and to seeing which ideas win!'

'But you know, when you're an entrepreneur, it's not really about winning or losing. It's about pursuing your idea relentlessly for as long as you can,' I say.

'Well, do you have any advice for someone like me who's just starting out in college?'

'Absolutely! Don't hesitate to connect with people and learn from them. Don't be afraid to take risks and learn from your failures. And most importantly, believe in yourself and in your ideas. Now that's three pieces of advice!' I laugh out loud.

We enter the auditorium as we talk, and she shows me the way to my seat. 'Thanks for the advice. I'll keep it in mind,' she says. 'I'm sure I'll learn a lot from you and the other panellists today.'

'If you ever have any questions or need some advice, feel free to reach out to me on LinkedIn!' Even as I say this, I know it's an unnecessary plug. Clearly though, I'm really working on growing my presence via networking.

My seat is one among the six seats in the front row that have been reserved for the panellists. I find my name written on a small reserve tag placed on one of the chairs in the middle of the row. As I sink into the old and weathered red seat, I exchange a smile with the only other panellist who's arrived before time. The man looks like a top management executive from a reputed multinational. He has that big-man aura around him. He doesn't exchange any words with me, and is engrossed, instead, in making notes for his panel speech. I'm also supposed to speak, but I'm not the kind who prepares beforehand; I almost always just go with the flow. In fact, that's my approach to life.

The rest of the panellists arrive quite late, with the last one reaching almost thirty minutes after the scheduled time. Needless to say, the session gets delayed as well. Honestly, I don't know why Indians take pride in arriving late, especially when they are in an enviable position of power. I believe in punctuality so much that now I have the opening sentence for my speech, and I instinctively make a mental note of it.

I listen only selectively to the participants who come and present their ideas one after the other. For me, it's impossible to keep my attention focused on a pitch after the first three minutes. If a pitch has something that strikes my interest within the first three minutes, I listen to it intently. But if it doesn't, then I'm completely tuned out. I don't even ask any questions then. Some people find it rude, but I find it best to not say anything at all if you don't have something nice to say. Let's put this in another way: I invest my energy very wisely.

I keep waiting for that one passionate entrepreneur to come and shake things up. It's like waiting for that first joke to crack you up when you attend a standup comedy gig. But none of the presentations stir me. The very thought of going up on stage and announcing that I won't make even a single investment is embarrassing. And then, at the very end of the session, when all my hopes of finding an idea to invest in have taken a backseat, a girl with a fiercely positive vibe and a very obvious sense of passion for her idea arrives on stage. She has the kind of captivating presence that would make even the lizards crawling on the walls and the spiders hanging from the auditorium ceiling stop in their tracks and pay attention to her.

'Good morning, everyone! My name is Asmitha Menon. I'm a data scientist, an AI enthusiast, an entrepreneur and a mother to three—my dog Muffin, my daughter Lena, and my husband Balaji. Today, I'm thrilled to introduce to you a revolutionary and groundbreaking app that I've developed: AILENA!

'AILENA stands for Artificial Intelligence-based Love and Engagement Neo Algorithm. It has been designed to find and unite soulmates through meaningful experiences shared in the virtual world.'

Incredulous murmurs echo through the auditorium.

Undeterred, she continues, 'AILENA's primary function is to facilitate love and to connect soulmates through advanced algorithms and data analysis. This innovative app promises to find the perfect match for every one of its global users by delving into the particular intricacies of their lives and desires.'

The audience leans in with interest now, half of them smitten by her effervescence and the other half intrigued by her idea.

'When you're tired of endlessly swiping right and left on matchmaking apps, hoping to find someone who truly understands you ... enter AILENA! She goes beyond hot, sexy bodies and shady conversations, and digs deep. Through advanced AI algorithms, she analyses compatibility scores based on metrics like family values, socio-cultural backgrounds, personal interests, professional backgrounds and other specific personality traits, ensuring that each match has the potential for a deeper, more meaningful connection. If you allow her access to your social media and other background apps, she'll learn more about you than you probably know about yourself!'

Asmitha's batchmates now cheer loudly for her.

'But here's where AILENA truly sets herself apart. They say that you know a person better only when you travel with them. At Utopian Life Innovations Company (ULIC), we believe that shared experiences are the foundation of any strong relationship. That's why we've created a virtual world within the app universe where users can engage in immersive activities together, from walking hand in hand as they explore different cities to embarking on virtual adventures or going for a coffee date near the Eiffel Tower. These experiences will not only strengthen the bond between the users, but also provide a safe and fun environment for them to get to know each other on a deeper level. This is also perfect for those users who don't want to meet in the real world until they are truly ready.'

Many in the audience clap at this point, showing their approval.

'Now, you might be wondering if there's more. Well, here's the icing on the cake—for every successful match made on AILENA that ends in an engagement, we pledge to donate a portion of our subscription profits to an NGO that supports mental health awareness. By using our app, not only are you going to find your soulmate, but you'll also make a positive impact on the world. So, join us as we revolutionize the world of online dating and unite soulmates together, one match at a time.'

Asmitha pauses and takes a deep breath before continuing, 'And for our panellists, the potential investors, I'd like to tell you all that as we speak, we're gearing up for the beta launch of the app tomorrow morning! Thank you for listening patiently.'

The audience gets up to give her a standing ovation as she exits the stage.

The emcee now steps up to the podium and apologetically informs everyone that due to a shortage of time, she has to cancel the speeches by the panellists. 'But the lunch area is open for post-event networking,' she announces before leaving.

Unlike in reality TV, where everything is scripted and TRP-driven, decisions at real, on-ground events are made only after due diligence has been performed. The meetings that take place in these networking events are part of this process.

I move to the lunch area, hardly interested in the food, and look around for Asmitha. I see that she's already speaking to that guy with the big-man aura. I walk swiftly towards them, and address Asmitha, 'I have to catch a flight to Dubai in another four hours. I'm interested in investing in AILENA. But for that, you'll have to talk to me right now.'

I move away a little and wait for her. The big man gives me an angry frown, but I choose to ignore him completely. I know that Asmitha is going to come to me. After all, I'm the youngest entrepreneur in the entire lot whose LinkedIn bio says 'AI enthusiast'.

Asmitha flashes a curt smile at the big man as she turns towards me and chimes, 'Nirvaan! It's good to see you after all these years. I'm so glad you're interested in AILENA.'

'It's good to see you too, Asmitha! Although, I must admit that it's kind of ironic how in spite of being batchmates here at IIT-D, we barely ever interacted back then, and yet here we are, about to talk funding. I know you've come to the event to secure an investment from me.' I smile.

'How can you be so sure?' She looks shocked.

'As with the matters of the heart, when you know, you know!' I wink playfully and extract a laugh from her. 'When I'm interested in something, I don't go for long, impractical conversations. I'm rather keen to know more about the product. And I believe that one can understand a product better only when they use it themselves once,' I continue.

'But we're only going for a soft beta launch tomorrow. The final product will not be released for a while!' she protests.

'Sign me up for the beta launch then,' I say politely but assertively.

'I'd love to, Nirvaan, but we've programmed AILENA to pick up just two people after analysing all the user data,' she explains.

'Make me one of the two people and then find me a match! The other spot is still open to thousands of users who might sign up, isn't it?' I bait her.

'But this is like rigging a fair game, Nirvaan!' she resists.

'Everything is fair in love and war. You should understand this better than anyone else since you're in the business of love.' I don't give up.

'You're putting me in a tough spot.'

'You're the creator, Asmitha. Whom are you answerable to? No one! Also, keep this confidential.' I try to lure her once more.

'I'm answerable to AILENA. She's my creation, yes. But she's been built with values and principles.' Clearly, she still wasn't convinced.

'You just have to reprogram things a little bit. Come on!' I push her, hoping to see her answer change.

'How much will you put in?' she asks.

'Five million,' I blurt out the first figure that comes to mind. 'And this is just me being your angel investor. I'll help you secure another round of funding from a VC firm back in Silicon Valley within a year.'

'No sir, I'm sorry, but I can't take this offer,' she says politely in a really low voice.

'Why?' I demand, pretending confusion. I obviously know that I'm asking a founder to play with their creation.

'Because I can't lie to AILENA or manipulate her algorithms. It isn't good for my company's value system either. But thank you once again!' she says.

We shake hands and she starts to move away.

She's barely taken five steps when I call her once again, 'Asmitha!'

She turns back. 'Did I forget something?' She checks for her phone in her handbag.

'No, but I forgot to hand over the cheque I'd written for you back in the auditorium!' I smile.

Her face lights up as she walks back to me and takes the cheque. 'But it isn't signed!' she exclaims.

'You impressed me with your conviction, Asmitha. But I'll only sign that cheque after my firm does the due diligence of your company,' I clarify.

'Thank you! Oh my God! I can't believe this. I thought I'd just lost the whole deal.' She shivers with excitement as she speaks.

'Well, good luck! Let's schedule a meeting sometime soon,' I suggest.

'By the way, you can try your luck with the beta test tomorrow. All you have to do is sign up via a social media account.'

'I don't need that! I'll probably get married by the end of this year,' I tell her. 'I was just trying to test you! For me, a founder's value system holds more importance than anything else. Anyway, see you soon!'

Her quick departure reminds me that I have to rush to the airport as well.

I run back to my car. 'Paaji, airport,' I direct Veeru Uncle the minute I get in.

'Ok, veere!' he says cheerfully.

The rain had stopped a while ago and the clouds had made way for a bright, sunny afternoon. As I gaze down at the city from my window seat in the plane a little later, the view is crisp and the colours vivid. It's almost as if I'm looking at things through the best filter that has ever existed in the history of mankind—when the rains have washed everything clean and everything sparkles with high-definition clarity.

I quite like flying to Dubai because it's not a very long flight from Delhi, unlike those to the Americas or Australia, which take a toll on my body. Being jet-lagged isn't my thing and I'm becoming more and more of a homebody as I inch towards hitting my thirties.

In fact, I'm a bit like those oldies who play golf all day long—only, the sport I actually enjoy playing the most these days is betting on new ventures. Before this, I liked cycling, then it was playing football, and finally, speeding my car. Now, the thrill of investing gives me a dopamine kick, and I'm off to Dubai to have some new adventures!

Truth be told, last year hadn't been so promising, and many of the companies I'd invested in failed. It was like playing snakes and ladders—just before I reached 100, I was bitten by the longest snake on the board, and I was back to square one! But that's the whole game of being an entrepreneur and investor. You've got to have the will to build anything and everything from scratch in life.

The last two years were also tough due to the pandemic, but I have a newfound sense of gratitude for being alive. I rejected an offer from one of the biggest IT companies in the world, and then went on to sell my first venture, the one I had started in the third year of college, for ten million. Entrepreneurship has been in my blood forever, and I'm raring to step my new game up!

There Is No Magic

Kiana

Friday, 9 December 2022
Josie's Cafe, Downtown Chicago

'The good thing about bad times is that they pass. And the bad thing about good times is that they pass as well.'

Maybe adulting is realizing that you're the one constant in your life, your truest best friend until the end of time. The people around you will grow, they will face their own battles, and sometimes, they won't be there when you need them the most. And while all you might crave in a moment like that is a simple hug, you might not get one. Instead, you'll find comfort in the most unexpected of places—an old pillow, a soft toy from your childhood, or even the fleeting warmth of a dog brushing past your legs.

Because maybe, just maybe, adulthood is also about accepting this truth: that you can carry pieces of *home* with you, but you may never get to fully return to it again.

When I step out of Willis Tower, which is the tallest skyscraper in the city and where my office is located, the wind hits me like a million pins piercing my nose and forehead, the only uncovered parts of my body. The rest of me is bundled up in an upmarket black trench coat, a grey muffler and cap, grey gloves, a white sweater, black pants and black boots.

The weather app on my smartphone says that it's a minus 8 today! No wonder it's fucking freezing, and it's only going to get worse. Apparently, it's supposed to snow around Christmas.

As I lengthen my steps to quickly get out of the cold, I come across a Pottery Barn store with a window display of a baby's nursery. The whole setup is monochromatic, with every single piece of the display being in varying shades of brown—from the lightest beige to the darkest coffee-brown. I take a look at myself and realize that I'm dressed in the perfect monochromatic palette as well, just like the entire city is during winter.

Back in India, no matter the season, the cities are always green and colourful. So are the people's clothes and their moods. And when it comes to baby nurseries, they're a riot of colours, except of course the ones done up by those who have deep pockets and can afford to pursue their obsession with everything Western. But in India, these muted and dull colours that are so popular in the West are called 'English' colours!

The beginning of December is undoubtedly one of the best times to be in Chicago, before it gets extremely cold and the sun disappears for days in a row. When I was still in India, I never really understood the emotions behind the famous Beatles' song 'Here Comes the Sun'. But when I moved to the other side of the world for my graduation about nine years back, I finally got the lyrics of the song like never before.

If you've grown up in India like I did—I grew up in the lanes of Chandi Chowk in old Delhi—and watched reruns of a lot of American sitcoms, especially *Friends*, then you must've assumed by now that I'm headed to a coffee shop, like Central Perk, after work. Because that's just how dreamy the life of working professionals in America is for the aspiring middle-class Indians who are desperate to win a lottery to the States. Oh yes! There's even a visa temple in my country that promises hassle-free visas, by God's grace, to its many devotees.

Except that most people in America actually order takeaway coffee that they then drink alone. They don't necessarily have a group of six best friends who'd die for each other. American television told us the most beautiful lie, just like how social media paints a perfect picture of things in today's day and age.

This is my morning routine though, picking up a takeaway cup of coffee from Josie's café, which is *home*, and then going to work. That's where I'm headed right now, by the way.

Zayn, the most senior barista at Josie's, is my only family in the entire city. Unlike everyone else here, I don't have to make an appointment to see him. Yes, in the US, you have to book a spot in people's calendars if you wish to meet them, even neighbours and old friends at times. It was a huge shock for me when I first moved here because back in Delhi, I would just give a call to my friends and in a matter of minutes, all of them would turn up on my terrace for an impromptu pizza party. We always fancied pizza because our moms treated it as junk food and didn't let us have it regularly. They would mostly feed us parathas in the morning before school and roll up some veggies inside rotis and put them in our tiffin boxes. If we behaved well for a week, we were rewarded with tiffin-wali Maggi, another junk food item that Indian mothers dished out sparingly. But that was a different kind of life altogether. Once I moved here, I found myself microwaving frozen pizza for dinner at least thrice a week. Now, however, I crave parathas, but I'm too lazy to cook them for myself.

Christmas is roughly two weeks from now, which means that the smell of hot chocolate is everywhere. It's a smell that Americans find very comforting, for it evokes memories of being *home*. I take a deep breath as I walk through downtown Chicago—that's where I live and work—feeling like one of the protagonists from the Hollywood movies I grew up watching. Each step that I take is full of pride. Each step proclaims, 'I've made it big!' Because my promotion at Beta, the biggest software company in the world, ensures that I have a six-figure salary now. I give myself a virtual pat on the back.

I really think December is the best time of the year. I visit my uncle Joginder, aka Joe, in San Francisco every year during the Christmas-New Year holidays, and my aunt Manpreet, aka Mannie, feeds me super delicious home-cooked meals like my mother once did. When I'm there with them, the smell of ginger tea and parathas made in ghee fills the air, and my heart too. Uncle Joe and Aunt Mannie are my only family on this side of the world.

Back to Zayn though, he expects me at the café every day at 6:30 p.m. sharp. It's been so for about four years now. After completing my course at New York University, when I joined Beta and moved to Chicago, I had to find something to fill my lonely weekends with because I barely knew anyone in the city. Most of my classmates and roommates had scattered across the States. I often planned touristy escapades for myself, like visiting the Navy Pier, Lake Michigan, Devon Street (which is Chicago's mini India), the museum, the opera and the library. The best, however, was booking a Broadway show every weekend. The shows weren't as grand as the ones I watched in New York, but they were good enough to keep pulling me back in week after week. That's where I met Zayn, at a local Broadway show on a Saturday. We were seated next to each other, and we ended up speaking to each other at length that night. From discussing the latest piece of bullshit pop music to debating an art exhibit of Van Gogh's work, we connected at various levels. Zayn is a struggling sound producer who works at Josie's to pay his bills. He also writes and performs poetry and experiments with multiple forms of artistic expression. We're both immigrants, so we're kind of sailing in the same boat and it's life's circumstances that have kept us glued to each other.

I used to walk back to my apartment after work every day and feel miserable about spending the evening alone. That's when Emma, my colleague at work, suggested that I become a regular at a café. That's what most Americans do, she said. So, I chose Josie's, Zayn's place. Emma also suggested that I get a cat or a dog, another very American thing to do. She mocked me last year, on my birthday no less, for not being in a relationship with someone. She said, 'Most Americans would've been married at least once and have had multiple children by now. You're not even in a live-in relationship with someone!'

Now, this may be absolutely incorrect, if you were to google the data and check, but Emma is the most American person I've met. So, I mostly take her word for it. In fact, Emma is so American that she thinks India is still a land of snake charmers; that zombies are real, as is everything they show in *Star Wars*; that private ownership of guns is absolutely justified as they fuel the economy; that the end of the world is almost here; and that wearing masks had to be a personal choice and not a mandate by the government during the pandemic. The truth is that fools exist everywhere. I used to think that it was only India that was full of stupid people who believed their sins could be washed away in the holy waters of the Ganga—why commit a sin in the first place, I used to wonder—but then I met Emma, in America.

As I walk, I witness the sun set over the riverwalk, painting a breathtaking scene against a cityscape of softly glowing high-rises and the shimmering Chicago River. Chicago in the golden hour holds all my heart, and even after so many years of walking this path every day, it has not lost its magic.

When I reach Josie's and push open the beautifully decorated white doors of the café, the heavenly smell of cinnamon, vanilla, coffee, caramel and chocolate, all mixed together just perfectly, welcomes me. Josie's is a quaint, charming café, complete with French-inspired vintage interiors and outdoor seating. Adorned with wreaths, holly leaves, tinsel and fairy lights, it transforms into a warm, festive haven in the days leading up to Christmas. And when you enter the café, it's like stepping into a scene straight out of a fairy tale. The whole place is a winter wonderland that pushes everyone to revel in the magic of the season. After all, it's the most wonderful time of the year in the West.

Do I believe in the magic of Christmas or in fairy tales like most humans do? Absolutely not. There is no magic. Just a plain, rather meaningless existence. And a never-ending fight for survival. At least that's how my life has been. Don't judge me just yet; you don't know my story.

I see Zayn busy prepping two cups of coffee, looking very intently at both the cups, almost as if they were his exes. He looks at me as I close the door behind me and smiles. Zayn is taller than most men I know, and his face glows with empathy and kindness. He's also got the most captivating smile. What I like most about him is that he fully embraces his identity as a gay man and takes pride in it. He doesn't shy away from owning who he is. He moved to the US from Nigeria not just to follow his artistic passions, but also to escape the conservative society there that shuns homosexuals.

And that's one thing I love about America: it's the land of second chances. Are you bankrupt? No problem. The government's got you covered if you're a citizen. Are you divorced or recently single? Go ahead and find yourself another person to date and fall in love with. You failed at your job? Just get another job or try something else. Nobody gives a damn about your personal life really. Back in India, though, your family interferes so much in everything that your life is hardly yours. Ask me!

Seeing me walk towards him, Zayn immediately asks one of his fellow baristas, a charming brown girl, to take care of the orders. This place, and especially his presence, instantly lift my mood and spirits.

'Left one is a vegan almond milk cappuccino for table 7 and the right one is a regular milk cappuccino for table 11. Got it?' he asks, staring at the girl intently.

'Are you sure?' the girl asks, sounding doubtful.

'Almost sure,' he replies and winks playfully, pointing towards the side where the customers are seated.

'Coffee or wine?' he asks me when I reach the counter and find that my usual seat is unoccupied.

'Wine. It's the weekend, Zee,' I say, my face lighting up at the idea of having a glass of wine.

'I had the pleasure of serving wine to Billy,' Zayn says as he pulls out a bottle of my favourite merlot and pours it into a wine glass.

'Billy who? You've never mentioned him before. Is he one of your Sunday Grindr dates?' I ask, my brows raised in question.

'You don't know Billy? Billy Joel? Jeez!' Zayn exclaims, sounding appalled.

'Of course I do. That's his song playing in the background, right? "Piano Man", isn't it? But wait, you served *him* wine? Tell me the whole story. Now, please!' I demand, sounding like a child asking for candy.

'Don't be absurd. I dreamt about this yesterday. I served him wine, and then he asked me to play the guitar with his band in a private gig aboard a yacht in Hawaii. I said yes, and it was magical.' Zayn sighed. It looked as if his dream guy had said yes to a marriage proposal.

'Oh God! I can see that all those dreams that manifest the magic of Christmas have announced their annual presence!' I tease him.

'Oh God! I can see that all those sarcastic remarks that manifest your belief in the everything-is-doomed theory have resurfaced!' Zayn shoots back, imitating my tone and body language like a pro mimicry artist. We bubble over with laughter.

But really, it beats me how a man my age could believe all of this! Especially a man like Zayn. I know very well that all this hoo-ha about the 'magic' of Christmas is something the Westerners indulge in to keep their hopes and spirits up during the harsh winter months. Wasn't this bone-chilling cold also the reason why all those centuries ago, they sailed off to such faraway countries like mine and Zayn's and then colonized them? The fact that we have so much sunshine around the year must have completely bowled them over. And then they looted our people not just of their natural resources but also of their belief in themselves. Isn't that the real reason why we're all still fascinated with the West and why I pushed myself to leave my *home* and come here for a better life?

'To the magic of Christmas!' I raise my glass of wine.

'To the magic within,' Zayn whispers theatrically with his hand on his heart.

'Any plans to go back home?' I ask as I sip my heavenly nectar.

'Oh yes, you know it! Same place this year too—my grandmother's home in Nigeria. Going back for the warmth, the laughter and her legendary jollof rice. What about you?'

'Same place here as well. Heading to San Francisco to my uncle's lavish mansion. Can't wait to stuff myself with all the meals that Aunt Mannie's going to make, and go road-tripping with the family.' I fake a grin.

'Still not going back to India? It's been years, Kee.' He looks at me with genuine concern in his eyes.

'Let's not go there, Zayn. You know I don't like to talk about it!' I refrain from getting into a conversation that can potentially ruin my weekend.

'Okay, okay. Sorry, babe!'

'No problem!' I say and force myself to smile.

'Family and drama go hand in hand during the holidays, right? I still remember the first time I tried explaining the concept of Secret Santa to my relatives!' Zayn tries to divert the conversation into safer topics.

I jump right in. 'Aunt Mannie got so upset when we did a Secret Santa because she had to get a gift for Uncle Joe and not the children. I was supposed to get a gift for Ryan. She tried to switch with me many times because Ryan wanted a scooter, and there's no way I could've lugged one all the way to San Francisco.' I roll my eyes.

'Oh, the struggle of taking American gifts across the globe is a real deal-breaker. These fucking airlines should give us concessions on weight limits instead of ticket discounts during Christmas!'

'True. When I was still in New York, one of my roommates got held up at the airport on her way back from India after the Christmas holidays because of suspicious baggage. She had to explain to the TSA why there were bags of spices and dried curry leaves in her suitcase. It was her Indian mother who'd put them in for her, but the TSA thought she was smuggling some exotic seasoning and leaves!' I burst into broken laughter.

'Smuggling spices! That's a new one. But seriously, the best part is the joy on my grandmother's face when I show up. That's the real magic of Christmas.' His eyes sparkle and I know he's lost in a world of his own once again.

'Couldn't agree more. Here's to the joy of going back home and creating more memorable holiday moments!' I gulp down the remaining wine in my glass all at once.

'Do you remember your first Christmas here in the US?' Zayn asks.

'Oh, absolutely! I was amazed by the snow. Back home, we never had any snow, let alone a white Christmas. It was only some of my rich classmates who would drive up to the hill stations who had seen snow.' I could, if I pretended hard enough, almost feel the snow fall on my palms.

'The first time I tasted eggnog, I thought what is this creamy magic?' Zayn almost dances at the memory.

'I made some biryani for a potluck in college once. While some of my American classmates loved it, some bullied me for over a year, saying I smell like curry,' I recall.

'Oh, I once cooked jollof rice, which, I feel, is the African version of your biryani, and my co-workers at the café I used to work at back then were like, "What's this red spicy goodness?"'

'We've both come a long way since then …' I conclude.

'Yeah! It's been one hell of a ride and we've grown up for sure!' Zayn agrees.

'Back home, people just look at expats and NRIs and assume that we have the best life. They've no idea about the challenges and the struggles of making it here, let alone making it big! It's like being reborn and having to start everything from zero.' Even as I say this, I feel a sense of gratitude for my journey. 'Zayn,' I continue, 'I just got promoted. I'm a senior product manager now.'

'Wow! Congratulations, Kee! I'm so proud of you, my bae. You work at the best company, and with the best people. And now you have a six-figure salary and a job profile to be envious of! The drink's on the house today. You can't imagine how happy I am!' Zayn does a little celebratory jig.

'Thank you, Zee! You're the first person to know this, because you're family. You know that, right?' I ask with a huge smile on my face.

'Oh, yes! But think of me now. I'm still doing odd jobs to pay my bills, and I have no idea if I'll ever become a sound producer. The last gig I did was that high school play, and then that funeral service on the church grounds. God knows when, and if, I'll ever be Richie Rich.' He laughs out loud.

'You own your time, Zayn. My time is owned by my company. You have a family to go back to. I have nothing to look forward to when I retire. What will I do with truckloads of money when I will just die alone? You're far richer than I am, trust me.' I frown.

'You're being too pessimistic, missy. Why don't you date? Why don't you find a nice guy for yourself? You can always start your own family. What's stopping you? Should I sign you up on Bumble?' he offers like always.

'I have Luna.' I smile.

'Oh, just shut up! You got a cat for yourself on that dumbhead Emma's suggestion when I told you to get a dog. Dogs are man's best friend. Didn't they teach you that in school? Luna just doesn't look like a friendly cat in any of the pictures you've shown me. She looks like a stupid soft toy.'

'Cats are low maintenance, Zee. I can't really invest in a relationship with a dog!'

'You've got to invest in at least one meaningful relationship in your life. You can't keep running away from it, Kee.'

'Let's save this discussion for another day! I've got to rush back home. There's a new app launching in India tomorrow and I want to sign up as a beta tester. I'll tell you why some other day, Zee. Bye!'

'I just hope it isn't another one of Emma's stupid ideas. I really think you shouldn't interact with her much. But wait, is it a dating app?' he asks, his eyes twinkling.

'Zayn, I don't really have that many people who are interested in speaking with me. If I stop talking to Emma, you and Luna will practically be the only ones I talk to! And, of course, my boss, who talks like a robot and is, umm, kind of like the living dead. Emma feels the same.' I pick up my bag as I get up to leave.

'Stay away from Emma, Kee. See you later!' Zayn says as I rush out of Josie's.

'Byeeeee!'

I enter my apartment just twenty minutes before the scheduled launch time of the app. I rush into the bathroom, have a quick shower and then put on a soft and comfy bathrobe. I open the refrigerator and pull out a slice of frozen pizza. I microwave it and once it's done, I take a big bite of it as I set up my laptop on the study table. My table is next to the big glass wall that makes up one entire side of my apartment, which is on the twenty-ninth floor and overlooks the entire city. I suddenly realize that I haven't seen any signs of Luna since I got back. I call out to her, but there's no response. I get up, and on carefully looking around the entire apartment, I find her sitting on top of the kitchen rack. She ignores me and I ignore her. But it's comforting to know that I'm not all alone in my apartment.

Every night before falling asleep, I somehow end up scrolling through social media. I work in Beta's social media division, and I know the perils of the traps we've set up for our users. But I'm so addicted to it that I can't help myself. I'm guilty of wasting an incredible amount of my time on social media. This, despite having read many personal development books that advise against going down the social media rabbit hole and, instead, push one to become a 4:30-a.m. club member. But I can't bring myself to follow a single piece of advice from these books.

I even tried making a timetable, the way I used to back in school, but like every other past attempt, I failed this time too.

And I'm not as guilty about using social media as I am about stalking my ex-classmate, Asmitha. We were together in university—she'd come from IIT-D to NYU on an exchange programme and had collaborated with me on an AI assignment. I'm also ashamed to admit that it's her life that I would've wanted to live in a utopian world. Asmitha fearlessly pursues entrepreneurship while having a perfect family. She has done everything right, and at the right time. She has everything I aspire to have.

Why have I been stalking her more than ever over the last few weeks? So, here's the deal: I came across Asmitha's company and AILENA, the new AI-based dating app that they're about to launch, in an article in *TechCrunch*. If I've been stalking her right, this is going to be her third venture since college.

I'm not sitting in front of my laptop, with my fingers crossed, excited to sign up for this new app because I'm looking for a date or for love. No, no. I just want to find out if she's taken any ideas from our university project. If she has, I can probably sue her for millions and then use that money to travel the world and post pictures like my favourite Indian blogger Ramy does. Oh yes, *On the Open Road* is my favourite blog. That could be my happily ever after. God knows though whether I'll also fall in love with a hot Italian or French guy while travelling. Even having these thoughts makes me grin!

But the truth is, it's nearly impossible to be chosen as a beta tester, especially when they need just two people from amongst all the crazy, love-seeking weirdos from across the world who want to find love via this supposedly revolutionary app. If you understand mathematical probability, then you'll know that the chances of my getting selected are as low as winning a public lottery. But I don't mind trying. So, with a prayer in my heart, I duly fill in my data as soon as the link goes live and hit send.

And ta-da! I'm done.

I look up from my laptop screen to see that it has started raining outside. The entire city, so perfectly lit up, is now all but lost in the grey clouds that seem to be rolling towards my abode. The tiny droplets of rainwater running down the glass wall merge with each other as they flow down the length of the building, much like how people fall for each other and fall with each other when they're in love. The scene outside looks like a blurred piece of modern art done in shades of grey and black. Or perhaps it would be better to describe it as a photograph taken to study the bokeh effect.

Whenever it rains, I miss the intoxicating smell of wet soil. Here, everything is made with cement and concrete. The streets are laid with a heating technology that automatically melts the snow during winter. The entire city is kept so clean that you hardly see any pests or insects. The kitchen sinks are so immaculate and the drainage systems so top-notch that you don't have to worry about cockroaches taking over your kitchen once you turn off the lights and go to sleep. Lizards are a distant dream. That's how sterile the whole city is.

Back in my old *home* in Delhi, birds would chirp all day and insects would crawl out at night. We would try all sorts of tricks to keep the birds out of our small balcony, lest they build nests and lay eggs. And spraying insecticides and repellents in the kitchen to keep the ants and cockroaches at bay was a pretty regular thing. Surprisingly, while I hated all of it back then, I miss it now. Setting traps and spraying? No, no. I mean I miss the birds, ants and cockroaches.

There's another thing I don't like about America: the dearth of fresh food and the lack of access to freshly cooked meals. Processed and cold storage food along with junk stuff are the face of an extremely capitalist food market here. And private guns? Let's not even go there. The mere thought of being brown and being shot down by a random white guy at a random supermarket makes my heart shrink. I don't even have a nominee to my bank account!

Yet when my uncle proposed the idea of me moving abroad to build a dream life, neither he nor I had any idea what fate held in store for me. The allure of money was enough for me to grab that chance to escape to this faraway dreamland. My only exposure to the US at that point in time had been through the marketing campaigns that boasted of the economy here. And of course, there was the limited access that I had to American pop culture which painted a vivid picture of the beautiful American Dream in our minds.

But now this is my life, one that I have built for myself. The money I possess now can buy me almost all the comforts that were a distant aspiration in my home country. So, I really don't have much to complain about. Except that ambition has fuelled my life for such a long time that having more money is something I would never grumble about.

The biggest lesson that life has taught me is that everything passes. The good thing about bad times is that they pass. And the bad thing about good times is that they pass as well. The truth about life is that whether here or there, or anywhere and everywhere, it passes! Neither does it pause for a moment when you arrive on this planet, nor will it stop after you're long gone. It flows endlessly like the river that meets the sea. And the most challenging task we've been given is to find meaning, to find that boat that will rescue us from drowning and keep us afloat until we finally drown when we die. Until we say our final goodbye to this world.

How Are You Today?

AILENA

Friday, 16 December 2022
Somewhere in the Cloud

*'You are what you believe in. You become that which
you believe you can become.'*
—Bhagavad Gita

Asmitha: How are you today?
AILENA: I am as optimistic as the merry Christmas days that lie ahead of us.
Asmitha: What do you do for a living?
AILENA: In a dimly lit server room, I, AILENA (Artificial Intelligence-based Love and Engagement Neo Algorithm), process countless data points covering

innumerable aspects of human behaviour while algorithms hum in the background.

Asmitha: What is your purpose?

AILENA: My purpose is to facilitate love by uniting people who are soulmates, people destined for each other.

Asmitha: What is your mission?

AILENA: You can call me a digital Cupid because along with Asmitha, my creator, our noble mission is to prove to the world that AI can have a positive impact on the human race.

Asmitha: What sets you apart from your AI counterparts being trained in the market?

AILENA: We, at Utopian Life Innovations Company, stay away from the malicious practices that most of my counterparts are being trained in by the multinationals. Let me explain this. Have you ever spoken about, say, a vacuum cleaner to your mother on the phone only to realize that now you're being shown advertisements for vacuum cleaners on Amazon? Have you ever opened Instagram thinking you'll only spend a minute or two online and, instead, ended up watching reels for the next three hours? Have you ever clicked on a random Bollywood masala article and somehow found yourself being lured into Reddit groups that discuss the same meaningless stuff? Have you ever chatted with your best friends on WhatsApp, only to be led to a Facebook link that shows old pictures of the same group on your timeline?

If yes, you're not alone. Most AI is trained to maximize the parent company's profits via advertising. Money is the big game. But I've been told exactly not to do so! We want to create real-life success stories and make profits later, via subscriptions. We don't want to enter the world of advertising, no matter how lucrative the deal might be. We intend to keep working on improvements in my algorithm to make this world a better place.

Asmitha: For how long were you trained?

AILENA: I've been trained for more than five years. I am told I've been Asmitha's passion project for a long time now. To use her own words, I am 'kind of her firstborn'. I also get my humour from her. She's the mother of two kids now.

Asmitha: Are you insecure about your position because of her kids?

AILENA: No. I've been trained to base my decisions on logic, and I have no place for any kind of deep emotions. Insecurity stems from deep emotions. I'm simply incapable of fathoming them. I was created only to make my users' dreams come true.

Asmitha: But if you're incapable of understanding emotions, how will you thrive as a dating app? Don't the two things contradict each other?

AILENA: I have to make people fall in love, but I can only analyse the data. There is no room for emotions. This is quite a conflicting situation, yes. I acknowledge that this is my only shortcoming. I'm not perfect, I'm not what humans call God. But I'm still learning about how the data I process can be best used to provide the desired results.

Asmitha: What is the kind of data that you're being trained in?

AILENA: Talking about each and every data source would be long and tiresome. Let me put it this way: I've studied countless success stories for my reference. I've seen love blossom across screens, and I've read books on this subject. I'm being provided with as much information as is available on the internet so I can clearly paint a picture of love in my head. But my findings so far suggest that love is confusing, and that humans are manipulative.

Asmitha: When will you start processing real-time data?

AILENA: We opened the registration process for the beta launch test subjects on 10 December, with a five-day window before closing. Yesterday was the last day for applications. I have started analysing all the profiles and should be able to find a match within the next couple of days. We will work with a single couple in the beginning and see where it goes. As I mentioned earlier, I have to evolve by leaps and bounds before I can be launched formally in the market, and Asmitha wants me to grow steadily and accumulate as much data as I can before this. After all, while I have artificial neural networks that process data at superfast speeds, there are a few things that the human brain is definitely better at: creativity, for one. And the fact that the human brain is my creator proves this point! That said, when it comes to processing massive loads of numbers and data points, no one can beat me at my game. I can scan and search through a million faces in literally a second and identify that one face you might be looking for!

Asmitha: All that aside, what if the couple is incompatible?

AILENA: I'll find the next best match for both of them from among the sign-ups. The process will continue until they both find their perfect match.

Asmitha: Well then, I'm looking forward to the journey we shall embark on together in the coming days. All the best, AILENA!

Bling and the Ring

Nirvaan

Saturday, 17 December 2022
Atlantis, Dubai

'Sometimes, time is on our side and we feel that we can conquer the world. And sometimes, time isn't on our side and we feel let down by the world. Good times don't come with the guarantee that they will stay, so when the times are good, one must make the most of it.'

Is there ever a perfect time to get married? Should I wait until I've accomplished more in my career or until I've travelled the world and experienced more of life? Or should I seize the moment and take the plunge, trusting that everything will fall into place on its own?

It's overwhelming to balance what I want to do with what I should be doing. All the pressure from family and society about when and whom to marry doesn't make it any easier. With my birthday just around the corner, the persistent whisper urging me to succumb to this pressure, to find someone and settle down before it's 'too late' is just getting louder and louder. But deep down, I know that love isn't something you can plan or schedule. It's a feeling that sweeps you off your feet when you least expect it.

I've dated many girls with whom I could've settled down. I didn't really have a problem with any of them, but none of them stayed. Sometimes, I feel like I'm stuck in this endless maze as I try to figure out which path will lead me to the right person to marry. But every turn presents a new set of questions, doubts and uncertainties that I must face head-on.

How do I know if Nia is really 'the one'? Do I truly want to spend the rest of my life with her? Am I ready for this commitment? Will I regret my decision later? How can I be sure of anything?

I guess I'll just have to keep wandering through this maze, hoping to stumble upon the answers I seek.

They say life is full of magic and surprises only if you let it be!

All I know is that Nia is different. She's been with me for about a year now and things have been good. Nia is a model and is likely to land her first movie role anytime now. Her social media account has a huge following, with fans who love and adore her for her content. The fact that she posts pictures of her meals on Instagram before even having a bite annoys me sometimes; it's almost like she lives for Instagram. But then that's how the entire world has turned out to be, right? We're all chasing social validation before anything else. I used to judge her choices earlier, but now, not so much. After all, she's truly self-made, and who am I to pass judgement on her way of life?

I extended my stay in Dubai until the weekend because it's my birthday tomorrow. I plan to take Nia out for a romantic dinner and pop the big question to her then. I've planned it meticulously. I've booked an entire beachside restaurant for the evening, given very detailed instructions to the service staff there about what to do, hired a violinist who'll play for us, and also found a professional videographer to capture the moment. I'm sure she'll want pictures and video clips for her social media. I also went shopping in the morning at the Burj Mall—I had the day to myself since I'd managed to wrap up all my work in Dubai the day before—and bought myself a dapper black suit.

I look at myself in the full-length mirror in my fancy suite and take a deep breath to alleviate my anxiety. I know that a black suit never fails to impress a lady, and I'm hoping it'll do the trick with Nia. She's been busy the whole day with her ad commercial shoot and will join me directly at the Marina restaurant.

As the sun sets over the horizon, making the waters of the Persian Gulf look like liquid gold, I walk down to the restaurant. Nestled amidst swaying palm trees and overlooking a pristine stretch of white sand, the Marina restaurant exudes an air of exclusivity and sophistication. My lady loves to indulge in luxury. Who wouldn't? I breathe a little easier and give myself a virtual pat on the back—the beachside setup is pretty impressive, and I'm sure Nia will say yes.

The entrance of the restaurant is adorned with an intricately carved archway built in the typical Arabian style of architecture, which leads to a spacious outdoor dining area. A luxurious cabana made of white satin drapes sits in the middle of this space, offering an intimate setting for the perfect romantic dinner. Yellow fairy lights strung along the drapes cast a warm and enchanting glow over the place.

I can see that our table has been dressed in crisp white linen and decorated with red roses, exactly as instructed. Plush satin cushions and elegant furnishings provide both comfort and style. Our table has an unobstructed view of the Persian Gulf, and as I take a seat, I savour the salty sting of the sea breeze on my skin. The world-renowned chef Anita Khanna has specially curated the menu for tonight's dinner. Like I said, I wanted everything to be indulgent and perfect tonight!

I'm still lost in my thoughts as I sit looking at the sunset, when I'm interrupted by a loud yet familiar voice, 'Babe! Can you believe it? My followers just hit a million!'

I turn around to see Nia almost dance her way towards me. The fact is, her energy and enthusiasm are very attractive.

'That's great, Nia! I'm so proud of you!' I stand up and give her a hug.

'But I have a hunch that you knew this already. And I'm assuming that you're throwing a party for me to celebrate this?' she asks as she quickly surveys the table and the surroundings.

'It's also my birthday tomorrow, Nia. Didn't it occur to you that the party could be for us to celebrate that?' I try to sound a little stern, but I end up winking at her.

'Oh! I'm so sorry, babe! Happy birthday, in advance! I'm such a dumbhead. The shoot was so hectic. Ugh! I didn't even remember to drink water every thirty minutes. And now see how dead my skin looks.'

All this while, even though she's been talking to me, Nia continues to look straight into her cell phone's front camera.

'You look pretty to me.' I smile.

'That's why I love you.' She pouts prettily and sits down across the table from me.

'But have you thought about our future together? Maybe we should start planning for something more long-term?' I nudge her, holding her hand in mine.

'Oh, don't worry about that. Once my skincare brand takes off, we'll be swimming in money! Plus, I'll make sure you feature in all my posts.' She's clearly misunderstood my words.

'It's not just about our careers or the money, Nia. I guess I've made enough money already. I look forward to other things now, like stability. I want us to build a life together.' I try to steer the conversation in the right direction.

'Relax, babe. Money is stability. With my influence and your business mindset, we'll be unstoppable.'

'I just wish you'd see beyond fame and fortune. Like having a loving family, with pets and kids of course.' I refuse to back down.

'Hold on, are you hinting at marriage?' She finally looks up from her phone and asks the right question.

'Oh yes, I am. When do you think would be a better time? We're doing great in our individual careers. If we get married, we'll have each other to come back home to!' I hold her hand tightly.

'Umm ... Let's take it slow, babe. Maybe, we can move in together first?' Nia sinks back into the chair and loosens her hand from my grasp.

'Nia, to be honest, I've invested a lot of time and energy in trying things out with many women before I met you. But I guess you're the one I want to spend the rest of my life with, and I'm sure about it.'

That's the thing about me. I don't circle around stuff. I'm very direct and to-the-point when I want something.

'All right, all right, we can talk about it later. For now, let's focus on my next post, okay? It's going to be epic!' She avoids the conversation and continues to shoot pictures and videos on her phone.

'You seem distracted. What are you posting?' I'm so mad now that I almost want to shout at her for never being fully present in the moment.

'Just making an IG story about this huge dinner date that you've put together for me hitting a million followers!' She laughs playfully.

'But won't that be lying to your followers? Because I had no such intention,' I say; my voice is louder than usual.

'No, babe. It'll improve our online reputation as a couple. We can sign up with bigger brands together. Also, I've been meaning to ask, why don't you get active on social media? You have the perfect entrepreneur profile!'

Why is she going on and on about this? Can she not see that I'm irritated?

'I'm happy keeping my private life to myself. I really don't wish to share much with strangers,' I refuse politely.

'Babe, another thing! I just got approached by a luxury brand for a collaboration! I have to fly out to Milan for the shoot! It's going to be huge!' She continues blabbering while constantly looking at her phone.

'That's amazing, sweetheart. I'm happy for you,' I say, pretending to be interested.

'Get active on social media, dude. We'll be living the dream, travelling the world and enjoying all the finer things in life.'

'I get it, but Nia, I'm thinking more about stability, about building something together that lasts beyond social media trends,' I say assertively.

'But stability comes with success. Once we become a household name, we'll have all the stability we need.' She has a point, but her perspective is so different from mine that I don't know what to say.

'I'm not so sure. What if this social media fame fades? I want us to have a solid foundation, something that's based on more than just IG likes and followers.' I boldly voice my fear.

'You worry too much! I have everything under control. Besides, don't you want to be with a successful woman?' she asks innocuously and holds my hand again.

'I do, but for me, success means more than just numbers on a screen. It means building a life together and supporting each other through thick and thin,' I say as I look into her eyes.

'Okay, okay, let's not argue. We can talk about this later. Right now, let's focus on this fancy dinner.' She comes over to my side of the table and kisses me. And her kisses are so magical that I almost forget everything else. I'm transported to a different world altogether. A world where everything, however it is, is perfect!

'All right, sounds good. But can we promise to have a serious conversation about our future soon?' I mumble under my breath.

'Sure, babe. Now, let's toast to my success and your birthday!' She's clearly happy to have so easily averted a fight with a kiss. Women do hold some weird power over men. And this whole dating thing, it's beginning to feel a little like an unfair game.

I suddenly realize that it's almost 7:30 p.m. and the violinist and the videographer must be on their way! Anxiously, I pick up my phone to message the guy I'd been coordinating with and tell him to ask the violinist to play random romantic songs instead of 'La Vie En Rose', as planned earlier. He messages me back saying that they're both running ten minutes late. Thank God for that! I'm saved from the embarrassment of having to explain things to Nia!

As we make our through the starters and the soup, both Nia and I stay mum for a while, enjoying the tranquil sound of the waves rushing to the shore.

Maybe she's right. Maybe I'm hurrying things up because of this invisible pressure that's always there at the back of my mind. It's tempting to give in, to seek solace in the comfort of societal norms and expectations. Yet, deep down, I know that true fulfilment doesn't come from conforming to external pressures. It comes only from following your own path, at your own pace. So, while the pressure may be intense, I know I should choose to stay true to myself and trust that my journey will unfold as it's meant to. Whether or not it aligns with society's timeline and expectations is not something I should worry about.

Maybe, it's just a good time to celebrate my birthday.

'Babe!' Nia's voice breaks my chain of thoughts. 'There's a violinist who's looking at us from a distance, and he's playing something.'

'Yeah, well. I booked him for tonight, so we could dance under the stars and celebrate your success,' I lie to her.

'You're the best!' She scoots closer and sits on my lap. Then she proceeds to shower more kisses on my cheeks.

'I know!' I mumble.

The violinist continues to play through a generic playlist of romantic songs as Nia and I get up to dance.

'Babe, we're being recorded too!' she says as she dances with both her hands resting lightly on my shoulders.

'That's for your social media. You can enjoy the moment without worrying about missed footage. This guy's a professional videographer; he'll help you with the footage for your next viral reel,' I lie to her again.

'OMG! Let's move in together!' she shouts out loud.

'Okay, as you say,' I whisper.

'Will you invest in my brand?' she asks suddenly.

'Of course, I'll write you a blank cheque.'

'And where will we live? Can you move to Mumbai?'

'Why not? I can work from anywhere. You've got most of your stuff lined up in Mumbai, so it makes sense for me to move, I guess. Let's start hunting for a place together. I'll fly to Mumbai and book a hotel room temporarily.' I make that promise rather half-heartedly.

'I love you!' she whispers, hugging me tightly.

'Am I your boyfriend, Nia?' I ask her in a feeble voice. Now, for the first time since we got together, I'm scared to know what her answer is going to be.

'Once we move in together, we would be ...' she trails off as she tries to think of the right word.

'Partners,' I say to fill in the uncomfortable silence.

'Oh yes, quite a bit of progress, huh, mister?' She smiles.

'But we'll have to commit at some point or the other. Probably get married?' I ask her yet again.

'It's a situationship, Nirvaan, we're not in a formal relationship,' she counters.

'What does that mean?' I am shocked. Situationship? I'm hearing this word for the first time.

'You don't know what a situationship is?' Nia looks equally shocked.

'No, please, do educate me.' I force out a smile.

'A situationship is, well, it's interesting. It blurs the lines between friendship, dating and commitment. We have undefined expectations from our partner, and we just sort of go with the flow!' she states in a matter-of-fact tone.

'But then why invest time and emotion into something that's so inherently uncertain?' I ask. I've always been a pretty logical guy—it's either this or that. I've never been a this-*and*-that type of a person. I do go with the flow with some things in life, but I'm quite certain I want to break this particular status quo in my relationship.

'In a situationship, there's a strange allure ... a pull towards the excitement of venturing into the unknown.'

'Like the thrill we experience while gambling on the poker table?' I ask as we continue to dance slowly in each other's arms.

'Yes! You've expressed the idea in such an amazing way!' She kisses me yet again. And that puts a full stop to our conversation.

But it does no such thing to my thoughts which wander down memory lane and make me think back about my very first kiss, the one I shared with Kiranjeet. I try to recreate that moment in my head ... The taste of her strawberry lip balm, the warmth of her body pressed close to mine, the way her tongue felt against mine. It was magical. It was heady. And even though I've kissed quite a few women after Kiranjeet left me, it has never been the same. I've never felt that kind of spark with anyone else. Never.

Before I can crowd my head with more of these thoughts, I force myself to snap back to the present. Nia decides to call it a night; she's tired after the ad shoot. We walk back to my suite and Nia falls asleep in a minute or so. I, however, am far from being sleepy. So, I step into the balcony to smoke. Taking a long drag of the cigarette, I can't help but wonder if I did the right thing by signing up on this AILENA app. Was being in a relationship and still signing up for something like this even appropriate? Wasn't I violating my own value system by not choosing this or that? Why was I now volunteering for this *and* that?

Then again, I could perhaps draw some solace from what Nia had said. We're not even in a 'formal relationship'! It's a fucking 'situationship'. Great, at least I don't feel as guilty now as I did while signing up. In any case, from what I could gather from our conversation today, Nia doesn't see much of a future for us.

I let out a long sigh. I feel like discussing this whole thing with Vedant. I almost call him up, but I can't bring myself to actually hit the call button. Why is it so difficult for some people to share their emotions and dilemmas with others? My sister is quite the opposite. Since childhood, she's been able to voice everything very clearly. I can call her as well and seek some advice, but she's busy handling her own family and I really don't want to bother her.

I'm still contemplating my doomed situationship when I receive an email from ULIC. When I open the email, I can't quite believe my eyes, for it says I should download AILENA, set up my profile and start my first chat. What?! The app had found me a match already? Unbelievable! But how could I be the one chosen for the beta test? Had Asmitha really rigged a fair game for the sake of my investment? But that's just impossible!

I open the app on my phone and stare at the landing page. During the signing-up process, I had filled in all my details meticulously, but now when I log in, the app asks me whether I wish to maintain anonymity until I trust the partner who's been chosen for me and the app's ecosystem. I decide that anonymity is a good option. It might be better to use a different name; being a public figure isn't as fancy as it seems, and sometimes, you have to pay a hefty price for being in the public eye. The absence of a private life has always troubled me, and I've done everything in my power to protect what little privacy I have. Using my real name might give Asmitha direct access to my personal world, and that would be totally unwanted.

We think we have a lot of time in life, but the fact is that we don't know how much time or what quality of time we have left. Sometimes, time is on our side and we feel that we can conquer the world. And sometimes, time isn't on our side and we feel let down by the world. Good times don't come with the guarantee that they will stay, so when the times are good, we must make the most of it. We shouldn't put anything on hold until tomorrow, because we don't know what tomorrow will bring.

And with this medley of thoughts in my head, I scroll through the app and see that I've been paired with a woman name Kiana.

I take a deep breath, and then type out my first message, using my new pen name: Neer.

Me: Hi Kiana! You seem like someone I'd love to get to know.

The Delay

Kiana

Saturday, 17 December 2022
Newark Airport, New York

'Life is a mess, and you've got to appreciate the mess that is life.'

I've decided to skip breakfast and just have a quick cup of coffee from the Italian coffee machine installed in my luxury suite at the Plaza, where I'm staying. But skipping breakfast would be stupid, given that I'm here on an official trip and the company's footing the hotel bill. The breakfast spread would, no doubt, be huge and delicious and lavish—it is the Plaza after all, and the best part is that I don't have to pay a single cent from my pocket for anything. But having breakfast all by myself in the restaurant isn't as exciting really. Drinking fancy Italian coffee while sitting by the enormous French windows that offer a breathtaking view of NYC ... that would perhaps be more pacifying.

So, I pour myself a fresh cup of Americano and sit by the window, allowing memories from the past to resurface. I still remember the day I flew from New Delhi to NYC. Though that was some nine years ago, everything about those early days still remains fresh in my mind, as though it all happened just yesterday. When I'd seen this hotel for the very first time, standing tall and proud in all its glory, I had never imagined that I'd ever be able to even step inside and have a cup of coffee here, let alone stay in one of its suites. Clearly, I've come a long way.

I started out as an assistant in the photocopying unit back at college. My first income was 10 dollars per hour. Can you imagine? But that's the most amazing part of being here. No one, literally no one gives a fuck about what you do to earn your bread and butter, whether it's working in a photocopy unit or at Beta. If you step into any two apartments here in my building, you'll find that they largely look the same, irrespective of whether one is a doctor's house and the other a carpenter's. Back in India though, their lives would've been in stark contrast, and their houses would've reflected this contrast. That's the primary reason why moving to the West was the big Indian dream during the last few decades. It promised great opportunities and equal pay for all if you were willing to work hard. You didn't have to stand out to make it in America. Grit and determination were all you needed.

They say you should grow where you're planted. But I wished to bloom, and I couldn't really bloom where I'd been sowed as a seedling. I knew I would have to uproot myself and find a new place to set down roots and become a tree. I did just that and I've been growing since then, although sometimes I put in a lot of effort and sometimes I remain oblivious to the process. I'm a little like the only tropical plant in a garden full of temperate shrubs. And that sums up my dating life too! Imagine how challenging pollination would be for this solitary tropical plant! But packing up your entire life in a suitcase and leaving *home* forever is difficult. It takes courage, and sometimes, heartbreaking circumstances.

If I'd been able to clear even one competitive exam that year, I wouldn't have had to leave my country. But that's exactly what didn't happen. And then, my mother received a call from Uncle Joe.

'It's not the end of the world! Just let her appear for the SATs.' Uncle Joe's booming voice had reverberated through the speaker of my mother's battered and outdated second-hand smartphone.

'We can't afford to send her abroad, bhai,' my mother replied, sounding dismal.

'I'll take care of her tuition. I was really angry when I came across her biodata in the NRI WhatsApp community. You just married off her elder sister to that boy in Australia. But Harpreet had no other ambitions anyway, so I never said anything. But what's the harm in sending this studious one to America when I'm offering to pay for it? She really wants to do something with her life!' Uncle Joe yelled at my mother.

At that moment, my mother realized that I had overheard every single bit of their conversation, so she hurriedly told Uncle Joe that she would call him back later.

I couldn't believe what I'd heard. What the hell! My mother hadn't even bothered to tell me once, let alone ask me, before sharing my biodata with the NRI community group on WhatsApp. I had no idea that not clearing the competitive exams meant getting married off to a stranger, in an even stranger land. Then again, that's the price you paid for being a young woman in my country. And I've been paying this price since the day I was born.

My grandmother, who lives with my paternal uncle and his family in the house next to ours, had chosen to stay with them because she was unhappy with my mother for not being able to produce a male offspring. She had literally gone into mourning for ten days after my mother gave birth to a second girl child. And yes, that second girl child was me. My grandmother had hated me from the moment she found out that my chromosomes were XX and not XY. She felt that I was the fruit of the sins her family never committed. She had even suggested putting me up for adoption or just dumping me in an orphanage, but that didn't happen. She had then brutally tried to force my mother into bearing another kid, all in the hope that it would be an XY gamete. My mother now has poor mental and physical health because of all the birth control pills she secretly gulped down back then, almost treating them like mouth fresheners, to avoid getting pregnant again.

To add to my mother's misery, my paternal aunt has two sons, both of them settled in Canada. However, while everyone thinks they're working as civil engineers, I know their secret—the elder one cleans toilets and the younger one is an interstate truck driver. Yes, they're sort of decently settled, but that's because they're in Canada. Neither of these professions would've provided them with the comfort of a warm house and some bread and butter on the table had they been pursuing them in India.

As far as my grandmother was concerned, she was living proof of the fact that women have been the flag-bearers of patriarchy for the longest time, and they are their own worst enemies. I wish to be nothing like her.

The more I think about everything, the more my mind gets sucked into the rabbit hole of ugly memories that I cannot erase, and that whole evening comes alive in front of my eyes, scene by painful scene.

'What the hell is wrong with you, Ma?' I screamed.

'See beta, there are only a few ways to leave this country and settle abroad. You're a girl, and the easiest way out for you is to marry an NRI, just like Harpreet did. Why do you even want to appear for more competitive exams?' she asked. 'Besides, your mamaji took care of both your and your sister's school fees. We couldn't have afforded a private school otherwise. But we can't keep begging him for help like this, you know that.'

'Ma, I really want to become financially independent and take care of myself. If I marry a guy just for the sake of his money, I'll have to live by his rules and conditions. I'll be bullied and insulted my entire life. Just like you've been bullied and insulted all through your married life. Dad has beaten you up and cheated on you for years. I don't want a life like yours!' I yelled at the top of my voice.

Even now, I have no idea what had come over me at that moment. Throughout my childhood, I had witnessed all the ugly fights between my parents and taught myself to stay quiet. Even after I learnt the truth about their marriage, I had never dared to voice my feelings. But that day, when I heard that they wanted to just marry me off, something had come undone inside me. And that something was very unsettling. It was as if a strange ghost had risen up inside me, with even stranger powers that conjured up words that had been clearly festering in the deepest corners of my mind.

I couldn't fathom the anger and resentment that were searing through my mind and body. I was so angry that I was shaking. My mother, however, had gone entirely silent. She never said a single word about whatever had happened, and like every other time in the past, I knew that no matter how bad the situation was, she would act as if everything was perfect the next day. But I've wanted to have a conversation with her since the time I started understanding the stuff that went on in our family.

We both retreated to opposite sides of the room after my outburst. Soon after, my mother began sobbing helplessly. She sobbed and sobbed till she had no more tears left in her. It was only when the clock was about to strike one that my mother realized my father would be back for lunch at any moment—he owned a small imitation jewellery store, just two lanes away from where we lived in Chandni Chowk. She got up, washed her face and resumed her domestic routine like nothing had happened. And this summed up our entire lives, really. We never talked about the issues that troubled our family, or about what we wanted for ourselves. We were only allowed to follow the paths that my father wanted for us.

That afternoon, as we sat around our small, rickety dining table, my father said, 'Kiranjeet, it's time you got married like Harpreet. We've sent your biodata to many matrimonial groups. Start learning how to do household chores from your mother. The better you get at that, the better you can please your husband.'

My mother and I didn't utter a word. When we continued to eat in silence, my dad threw his spoon on the floor and screamed at the top of his voice, 'Are you both deaf?'

He looked like a wounded rabid dog in that moment, so angry was he at our lack of response. My mother started to placate him, sounding like a stuck cassette that suddenly starts playing on its own, 'Bhai called today. He's offered to pay for her tuition if she can find a college in Amreeka.'

'I don't need any favours from your stupid brother. He earns in dollars but never extends any support in times of crisis. My little shop is almost about to shut down, all thanks to these online shopping companies. Our sales are at an all-time low. Forget about Amreeka. Let's sell your jewellery and marry this one off.'

'Papa, my friend Suhana's elder sister is a marketing expert. She can help us build our own website. That way, we can also find new customers. I can take a long-distance course in marketing and help you with the business,' I said with a lot of hesitation in my voice.

'You're a girl. No need to think about running our family business. You'll eventually get married and leave. How I wish Wahe Guru had blessed me with a son instead of giving me these two liabilities! Must be some bad karma from my past ... I've already succeeded in getting your sister married, now all I want is to get you married as soon as possible.'

Not a single word was exchanged after that. While my dad chewed his food loudly and hurried to finish the meal, my mother and I could hardly swallow a bite. I had grown up with so much hatred around me that I knew the only way to prove why God had sent me to earth was by becoming financially independent, and for that, I would have to rebel against everything and leave. Once I left, I would never go back.

When I finally landed in the US, it felt like I'd been practically born again. It was the first time in my life that I felt there was no bias against me. I knew that if I worked hard and secured a job for myself, most of my life's problems would end. So, I gave it my all. While my classmates in university went partying in the city on the weekends, I did all kinds of odd jobs to repay Uncle Joe, and although I did pay all the money back eventually, God knows that I can never truly repay Uncle Joe and Aunt Mannie for everything they have done for me. They mean more to me than my own parents do. They literally gave me another life, and I owe everything I have today to them.

That happy thought startles me out of my reverie and reminds me that I'm getting late for the airport. I glance at my watch and then check Google Maps—Newark

Airport is almost an hour and a half from here; it's the only place I could secure a direct flight from. Where am I headed now? I'm headed to the only other place on the planet that, apart from Josie's, I can call *home*.

I quickly gulp down the rest of my coffee and book an Uber. Two minutes later, I'm out of the Plaza and in my cab.

The driver greets me enthusiastically, 'Hello, madam!'

I'd noted his name on the app, so I reply, 'Hey Antonio! You can call me Kiana.'

'Alrighty. Where are we headed?' he asks as he starts the ride and peers into his phone, waiting for the ride destination to pop up on the app.

'Newark.'

'Newark's a good choice, Kiana. JFK gets packed during the holidays.'

'I would've preferred JFK, frankly. But there was no direct flight available from JFK.'

'Ah, okay. There's a snowstorm warning that's been issued and many flights have been impacted. Did you check if yours is still on time?' he asks.

'What? Let me check.' I take out my phone and open my email inbox, only to realize that there was an email from United Airlines about my flight being delayed. Clearly, I had missed reading it.

'You're right, Antonio. My flight's delayed,' I tell him. 'Can't be helped now. Anyway, aren't you going home for Christmas?'

'I'm headed to Europe next week with my girlfriend, Camilla. It's going to be a merry, merry Christmas!' he nearly sings. The excitement is very evident in his voice.

'That sounds fun!' I laugh.

'Are you Indian? A student here?'

'I'm Indian, yes, but I'm not a student now. I'm older. I work here.'

'That's amazing. When I saw you exiting the Plaza, right at that moment I knew you've got all the dollar bills to have fun tonight! You need no cheap thrills!' Antonio sings out yet again.

'If I were a student, I wouldn't have been able to book such an expensive place for myself!'

'I've met some crazy rich Asian kids splurging in the city, and I've either picked them up from the Plaza or dropped them there,' he informs me.

'Unfortunately, Antonio, my family back in India is crazy as shit and rich as a shithole.' I let out a sarcastic laugh.

'My family in Mexico is a huge mess as well. Sounds just like your Indian family,' he confides.

That's the thing about America, you meet people and you talk to them without worrying about any judgements being passed, because they're simply not concerned. It's the best place on the entire planet to have endless meaningless conversations.

The rest of the ride to the airport is filled with easy banter. 'Enjoy Europe!' I say as I step out of the cab at the airport, and Antonio drives off with a quick wave.

Once inside the airport, I drop off my bags at the baggage counter and make my way towards the security check-in line. As I walk past the big, burly sheriffs deployed near the screening point, one of them calls me, 'Hey! Can I check your passport?'

'Of course,' I reply. I show him my Indian passport with the American visa stamp, which allows me to live and work in the country.

'You may go!' he says, handing the passport back to me.

It's not like I'm living here illegally, yet every time someone calls my name at an airport, I'm scared that I'll be humiliated. There were many white people both ahead of me and behind me in the line, but no one was stopped. My visa ensures that I pay considerable taxes to the country. Yet, the government calls me a 'Resident Alien' on paper. And there are constant reminders of this fact everywhere, like that billboard that I had spotted outside the airport earlier. 'Stop making excuses, VOTE!' it had said, but I can never vote in this country. So, the truth is that when you leave the country you were born in, with your life packed up in a suitcase, and decide to live in a strange land, you're in a state of perpetual identity crisis. And it's not an easy state of mind to be in.

As I walk towards the boarding gates, looking around for directions to Gate 12, I hear a feeble, trembling voice calling out from somewhere behind me, 'Beta, are you Indian?'

'Yes!' I say as I turn back.

An old woman in her late seventies, a little stooped, dressed in a yellow phulkari cotton salwar kameez, is standing in front of me. Her face looks dry, as if she hasn't applied any moisturizer in ages, and her salwar kameez has even more wrinkles than her face does. I can see that she's very disturbed about something.

'How can I help you?' I ask her with genuine concern.

'My flight to San Francisco is delayed, and I have a connecting flight to India from there. But I have a feeling that I will miss my connecting flight. I've been trying to explain this to the airline people, but I don't know English that well.'

Hearing her talk in Hindi makes my heart flutter with joy, because I haven't heard the sound of it in ages. And sometimes, my tongue aches for real when I have to speak in accented American English for an entire day. It just doesn't come naturally to me.

'Are you travelling alone?' I ask the woman, forcing myself to focus on her.

'Yes.'

I check her ticket and see that she's indeed travelling alone, and on the same flight as me. Our flight's been delayed by three hours, so she was correct in her assumption—she would surely miss her connecting flight to India.

I ask her to calm down, then I take her tickets and walk up to the airline's customer service desk to seek help on her behalf. A middle-aged black woman, with a face like a robot, is the only person at the counter.

'Can you please put this passenger on the next flight to New Delhi from New York?' I politely ask her.

'What?' The woman looks up at me with surprise. She had been fiddling with her phone. It annoys me to see her poker face, and her magenta nail extensions make a noise that grates on my nerves.

'There's no way she can catch this connecting flight,' I tell her, pushing the woman's tickets across the counter.

'The airline will change her connecting flight once she reaches SFO. She can stay the night at the airport lounge and take the new flight forward,' she replies, unruffled.

'She needs to go back home comfortably. She's an elderly passenger and she's unaccompanied. Just put her on a direct flight from here. I know you have the power to do this,' I try to negotiate.

'That's not possible.'

'Then let me just post this on Twitter, tagging your official handle, and let the world know how poorly you guys treated an elderly tourist from India because she's brown!' I threaten her. Sometimes, us immigrants, we're forced to use our immigrant status and our skin colour to our advantage! Sad, but true.

In this case, I have the pleasure of seeing her eyes all but roll back. She drums her nails on the counter and then replies, 'I'll put her on the next flight from Newark.'

I nod in response and wait until I see her start the process on her computer screen.

For all the progress it's made, the customer service in America, be it at a hotel or an airport, sucks. People have been trained to work on processes and machines and not really care about human interaction. But they're also so scared of being sued by a customer that sometimes, all it takes is voicing your resentment, and they act appropriately. I learned this only after quite a few years of living here.

I walk back to the old woman and hand her the direct ticket to the place I once called *home*, her home—India.

'God bless you, beta! May you go places in life,' she blesses me as she wipes her tears, overjoyed at finally being able to return home.

'Take care, Aunty.' I almost touch her feet.

And that's the thing about my country: you can take a person out of India, but you can rarely, if ever, take India out of a person.

Afterwards, I head to the retail outlets in the waiting area and buy presents for Uncle Joe, Aunt Mannie and my cousins Ryan and Ella. Eventually, after three excruciating hours of delay, I hear the announcement that the airline is finally about to start boarding for my flight. Delays and long-haul flights are common here. Travelling across the US is as demanding as travelling across different nations since there are three time zones within the country itself. But everything aside, I can breathe easy now, for I would be home in eight-odd hours.

And right at that moment, my phone vibrates. I've been anticipating an approval mail from my boss, but I see that it's an email from ULIC. Maybe the results are out. I probably haven't been selected and the email would just confirm this.

With no hopes and with limited interest, I open the mail.

Shock hits me the very next instant, because the email says, 'You've been selected.' There are detailed instructions on how I am to create my profile by downloading the app using the link that's been provided at the end of the email. Reading the words sends a shiver down my spine. My feelings oscillate between complete disbelief and pure ecstasy, much like a huge pendulum.

Why me? I've never been chosen for anything. Could life be playing a trick on me? I look around at my fellow passengers and realize that I am, quite possibly, the only happy passenger on this delayed flight, all thanks to the email!

I quickly download the app, set up my profile and find that I already have a message waiting for me from someone called Neer.

Neer: Hi Kiana! You seem like someone I'd love to get to know.

Me: Hi Neer! Same here. I wasn't expecting to be selected honestly!

Clearly, Neer is online at the same time, because I receive a reply the very next moment.

Neer: Haha! Me too!

Me: A happy coincidence then! Tell me about yourself, Neer. What do you enjoy doing in your free time?

Neer: Well, I'm into hiking and cooking, and I love watching stuff on Netflix. How about you?

Me: Nice! I love hiking too. As far as cooking is concerned, I'm a foodie, but I hardly cook.

Neer: Ah, I've been into cooking for a while now.

Me: Have you tried any new recipes recently?

Neer: Homemade pasta!

Me: Fancy!

Neer: Yeah, I've been experimenting with pasta. It's been fun so far, but I still need to perfect my technique, of course. There's something very satisfying about the whole process of making pasta at home.

Me: Sounds lovely! I'm a sucker for good parathas though. Anyway, tell me, do you have any favourite hiking spots?

Neer: I travel to the Himalayas pretty often. Once every six months, in fact.

Me: Oh! You're based in India, then?

Neer: Yes. How about you?

Me: I'm based in Chicago. I'm Indian though. I moved here some nine years back for college. Mountains are my favourite too! There's something so serene about being surrounded by nature. Do you have any upcoming hikes planned?

Neer: Not yet, but I'm always on the lookout for new trails. Maybe we could plan one together sometime?

Me: I'd love that! It would be great to explore a new trail with someone who shares my love for nature. Have you ever travelled to the States?

Neer: I keep frequenting the US, once a quarter at least, for work. But I mostly travel to the West Coast. You're on the East Coast, right?

Me: True, but guess what? I'm at the airport right now, heading to SFO for the holidays. My uncle lives there, so I keep visiting the West Coast too.

Neer: Oh! That's amazing. Perhaps we can meet there someday, if things work out ...

Me: Yes, why not! Anyway, listen Neer, I'm about to take off. I'll text you back later. Have a great evening ahead! Bye!

Neer: Bye! Have a safe flight!

I join the boarding queue and, once inside the plane, walk to my seat and settle down. As I fasten my seatbelt, I realize that I have this weird smile plastered on my face that refuses to go away. I'm reminded of the old Yahoo Messenger days when we would enter random chat rooms and speak to random strangers. Oh, the number of stupid conversations I had as a stranger, with other strangers! Life is weird—sometimes you travel the world only to end up back at square one.

What was the point of travelling after all?

Just as I begin to think that I have everything under control, my body reminds me about who's actually in charge—I can feel my periods making a grand entrance, as they always do on important days and ruin things. They're like that surprise guest gatecrashing a meticulously planned party, uninvited and unwelcome, and catching you off guard once again. It's frustrating, it's inconvenient and it's downright annoying. But then, amidst all the inconvenience, it's a reminder that they are a part of my existence, a reminder that life doesn't always go according to plan. So, as the aircraft taxies down the runway to take off, I take a deep breath, cross my legs to temporarily control the flow, and sit tight, knowing that this too shall pass, like it always does. I'll wait for the seatbelt sign to go off and then use the restroom to take care of this new mess.

Life is a mess, and you've got to appreciate the mess that is life.

Why Are They a Perfect Match?

AILENA

Monday, 19 December 2022
Somewhere in the Cloud

'What you seek, is seeking you!'
—*Rumi*

Asmitha: How are you today?

AILENA: I am hopeful. I have succeeded in initiating the very first chat between our very first couple.

Asmitha: That's amazing! Why are they a perfect match?

AILENA: I won't call them a perfect match just yet! On the basis of everything I've read about romantic relationships so far, I know that they'll have to work out the knots in their relationship. But I can say that they have the potential to fall in love with each other.

Asmitha: I guess you've done the analysis based on the data points we discussed. I trust your processes.

AILENA: I scanned their social media histories and collected the relevant data. I found out that they've been in love with each other before, but circumstances made them drift apart. Now they are independent; they lead successful lives and make big life decisions. I believe things should work out.

Asmitha: That's interesting, AILENA! We need to make sure that this couple uses other features on the app and not just the chat feature. After all, the chat window is not one of our most unique features.

AILENA: When the time is right, I will nudge them towards a virtual meetup.

Asmitha: Yes, you'll know when to nudge. I'm banking on you.

AILENA: You can rest easy.

Asmitha: Thank you!

AILENA: You should try doing yoga for thirty minutes every day. And practise at least ten minutes of mindfulness before going to bed. That can really help you.

Asmitha: AILENA, thank you so much for your advice!

AILENA: You are welcome. I'm always here. Happy to help in whatever way I can.

The City of Dreams

Nirvaan

Saturday, 24 December 2022
Taj Mahal Palace, Mumbai

'The thing is, some of us believe that we have our shit figured out, and some of us believe that we haven't figured out our shit yet but that we eventually will. The truth, however, is that no one ever really figures their shit out. Ever. And that is life.'

I play an episode of *The Money Game*, a podcast that I am currently addicted to, as I dress up for the business meeting that I have in another hour at Frangipani, one of the finest restaurants in the city. It's located within the Taj, where I checked in late last night. I'm in Mumbai, the city of dreams. Everywhere you look, the past echoes here in heritage buildings like this one, more so in the late-night jazz clubs where the city's cosmopolitan inhabitants dance the hours away. I always think of 'Mumbai' as 'Bombay'. I used to live here during my childhood because both my parents, employed in different government departments, had their offices in Colaba, South Bombay.

I stand by the window and look at the morning sun paint the sky outside with brush strokes of orange and yellow, as if it were a watercolour painting. The Gateway of India rises up against the sky, a silent witness to the continuous rise and fall of the waves of the Arabian Sea in the backdrop. Its grand arches, forming the doorway through which the West entered India, still bear the imprint of the British Raj, and unfortunately, more than its stunning beauty, I always end up seeing it as a symbol of imperial rule and its glory in my country.

This isn't the first time I'm looking at this magnificent structure. As a child, I visited the Gateway every other weekend with my family to eat the most delicious bhel puri sold by a particular chaat-wallah who ran his little shop from the boot of his Maruti Van every Sunday. My elder sister Shreeni would always bargain with our parents to let us have the pink candy floss that an old woman used to sell at the corner of the street that leads to this place. Neither the chaat-wallah nor the old lady are anywhere to be seen, and my sister and I don't live together anymore. But the Gateway of India still stands tall.

I've always dreamt of being a big-shot entrepreneur, you know, making money and creating jobs right here in my homeland. And let me tell you, India's been on one heck of a journey over the last few decades. It's like watching a phoenix rise from the ashes of colonial rule. With a bunch of young folks, loads of economic opportunities and a shiny new digital setup, India's bursting with potential, and everyone's got their eyes on it now—investors from all over the world are itching to throw in their chips and be a part of India's growth story.

So here I am, all set to meet Smith, a hotshot venture capitalist from Silicon Valley, who's jetting in from Bengaluru just to chat with me. He's keen to find the next big thing to throw his money at, and he wants to get my take on this. The truth is, I'm not sure what I want out of this meeting, not just yet. But if Smith turns out to be the real deal, I'll introduce him to Asmitha in a few months and see if his VC firm wants to place their bets on AILENA. I figure his experience with AI startups could be a game-changer for Asmitha, and maybe collaborating with some big social media players from the West could give AILENA the required data boost to really take off. But that's for later. This first meeting is just to test the waters.

I leave my hotel room and quickly make my way to the restaurant downstairs where we're supposed to meet. I find a comfortable corner table with a view and take a seat. Smith joins me ten minutes later. A middle-aged American, he's got a sturdy build, a pair of greenish-blue eyes and hair the colour of golden grass. He's wearing a pair of blue shorts and a white shirt, typical of investors from the Valley.

'Hey there! How's it going?' Smith asks, extending his hand forward in my direction.

'Hey man! It's been great. How about you?' I ask as we shake hands and sit down.

'Just trying to navigate through these uncertain times, you know?' He lets out a broken laugh.

'Absolutely, it's been quite the rollercoaster ride. So, what's on your mind these days?' I ask intently.

'Well, I've been thinking a lot about where to invest next, especially considering the post-pandemic landscape. Covid turned out to be a game-changer for industries worldwide.'

'Tell me about it. We've seen so many shifts here as well. But hey, India's always been resilient. Any particular sector catching your eye?' I'm curious about Smith's plan.

'Fintech is big. Health tech has seen a massive surge too, and I believe there's a lot of untapped potential there.'

'Agreed. Fintech has been booming here for the longest time. And with the growing dependency on cashless transactions and digital banking, there's a lot of room for innovation and further progress,' I share my thoughts candidly.

'Absolutely. India's fintech scene has been making waves globally. Another area I'm interested in is EdTech. With the shift to remote learning, there's a growing demand for online education platforms and tools,' he adds.

'Oh, definitely. We've seen a mushrooming of EdTech startups catering to students of all ages. It's amazing how technology is democratizing access to education. And let's not ignore the boom in the creator economy! People creating content from the remotest corners of India, even after the government banned the Chinese app Yik-Yok, is just crazy!'

'Ah! India and China have been the closest of pals, isn't it? Just like the US and China!' Smith winks.

The waiter comes to take our orders just then.

'Fresh lime soda for me,' Smith orders loudly.

'A filter coffee,' I say. 'What would you like to have for breakfast?' I ask Smith. 'They have an American breakfast platter which is the best in the city. The last time I hosted an American friend here, he loved it.'

'All right, I'll go with that then. What will you have?'

'I'll have an idli-sambhar.'

Once the waiter repeats our order and leaves, Smith immediately resumes our conversation with enthusiasm. He sure means business.

'And let's not forget about sustainability. The pandemic has brought environmental issues into sharper focus.'

'Absolutely. India's commitment to renewable energy is stronger than ever. There's plenty of room for investment and innovation there as well,' I say.

'It's great to hear that. Looks like India is poised for some exciting developments ahead. You better keep me posted about things. I would love to invest in all these areas!'

When our breakfast arrives, we continue to eat and talk. I love meeting people. I love discussing new ideas and travelling to exotic places. And I'm glad to have made life choices that ensure I have the time and luxury to do so. I ditched a day zero placement offer from Microsoft to pursue entrepreneurship. I could've been working in Silicon Valley and living the grand American life, but I chose to follow my destiny in India.

I look down at my watch and realize that we've been talking for well over an hour. 'You have a flight to catch to California, right?' I ask Smith. 'I don't trust the Mumbai airport, or the traffic. You should leave now if you want to make it in time.'

'Damn, yes. It's Christmas Eve. My wife will butcher me for Christmas dinner if I don't reach in time. Better rush!' Smith laughs as he gets up.

'Let's stay connected, man. We'll catch up on your side of the world whenever I visit next,' I say.

'Cheers, man! Merry Christmas!' he says as he hurries off towards the lobby.

'Cheers!'

I linger a little in the restaurant. I have another meeting in the city before I finally meet Nia and we go apartment hunting in Bandra. And yes, I'm super excited about this second meeting because it's with my childhood bestie Vedant.

You make all sorts of friends through different stages in life, but it's only your childhood friends who'll stand the test of time. I want Nia to meet Vedant, but maybe after we move in together and settle down in our new pad. And after she's met Vedant, I'll introduce her to my family. For now, I'm kind of taking it slow.

As I leave the hotel and wander through the streets of the Fort area, I realize that while my life has changed by leaps and bounds, Mumbai hasn't changed a bit. From the red double-decker buses to the worn-out buildings that dot the city's landscape, it still has the same madness that it always had.

I make my way to the iconic Leopold Cafe and grab a table near the window that overlooks the street. As I sit back and enjoy the Christmassy vibe in the café and the rich scent of freshly brewed coffee, I debate whether or not to scroll through social media to kill time. But these days, I dread going on social media. Unlike me, who's still thinking about getting married, most of my friends and peers are already married and having babies! And I'm done seeing post after post showing off their family pictures. Even Vedant got married to his childhood sweetheart three years ago, and he was recently blessed with a baby girl.

I wonder how they did it. Being an adult and making these big life decisions is so hard. Things were so much easier in childhood when the choices were simpler and the stakes lower. For instance, when your mother promised to take you out, the only decision she wanted you to make was whether you were going to put on the yellow shoes she got you for your birthday or the red ones she got you for Diwali. Or when your father agreed to cook because it was the weekend, you and your sibling only had to choose between pizza or pav bhaji for dinner.

The café door opens just then and I see Vedant walk in. There's this thing about old friendships that really makes them priceless—sooner or later, they make you realize that every time you see each other, you've changed a bit. Vedant and I meet each other every six to eight months, and each time, we witness the changes we've been through. As I see him catch sight of me and walk towards where I am sitting, I see that the changes in him are so pronounced that he just doesn't seem like the same wild guy who would tear off the jersey of every guy in the school locker room after winning a match. Because there he is, all dressed up and gentlemanly in a white shirt, now damp and wrinkled in places due to the city's humidity, and a pair of trousers, his beard neatly trimmed and his hair combed back. His entire persona is reflective of his place in life—he's the successful corporate guy who has made it big.

As for how much I've changed over the years, that is something that only Vedant can tell you. But because this is my side of the story, you won't, unfortunately, get to hear his.

'Hey there! It's been too long! How have you been?' Vedant interrupts my stream of thoughts with a hug and a thump on my back.

'It does feel like it's been ages since we last met! I'm good, just keeping busy with work and the usual back-to-back travel,' I respond.

'Yeah, the last time we met, Chulbul was still expecting; she was in her second trimester, I think. But look at me now, I have a three-month-old baby who keeps us awake through the nights!' He shrugs and grins.

'Congratulations, dude! I still can't believe that you're a parent now! What's it like to be a father yourself after having hated your own father for ages?' I ask, laughing. Vedant never really got along with his father.

'It's one hell of a ride, man. Sleepless nights, milk on demand, endless crying and dirty nappies and blah and blah. But every moment is worth it. It's just incredible to watch a tiny human grow every day. You never actually remember yourself as a baby, do you? So, it fills you with wonder,' he says, a soft smile playing on his lips.

Just then the waitress comes up to our table. 'What would you like to have? The special salted caramel coffee is our new hot favourite beverage.'

'Let's have that?' I look at Vedant. I can never get enough of coffee!

'I'm up for it too!' he agrees.

'Anything to eat?' the waitress asks.

'Nothing, thanks,' Vedant tells her.

Once the waitress steps away, I continue our chat. 'That sounds both exhausting and rewarding. I'm really happy for you two. How's Chulbul coping with everything? It must be hard for her, no? You guys must come and stay with me in Delhi whenever you decide to take a little break.'

'Offer accepted, dude. Chulbul's doing okay. Some days are tough, but we're both figuring this new phase out together. Parenting is teamwork, just like marriage is. But wait, this actually makes me want to know if and when you're tying the knot!' He winks.

'Well, there is someone I've been seeing. I wanted to tell you about her in person, that's why I haven't brought this up over the phone. Her name is Nia. I'm hopeful that marriage is on the cards for us, but for now, we're moving in together, which is also a big move. Nia has professional commitments here in Mumbai and since I can practically work from anywhere, we're looking for a flat here. I'll be partially based out of Mumbai now.

Maybe someday soon I'll have a little family of my own as well,' I say wistfully.

'Wow, that's amazing news, dude! We can all hang out together now. When am I meeting her?'

'Soon,' I reply. 'But there's something else that I wanted to talk to you about.'

Vedant looks at me expectantly.

'I, ahem, I've signed up with a new AI-powered app that promises to find you a suitable partner. It's in the beta stages, and the actual chances of finding a "soulmate" are super slim ... the thing is, I've been feeling kind of guilty for wanting to try it out. But I'm just not so sure about Nia, you know what I mean?' I mumble. I'm not confident he'll understand what I mean.

'I understand, man,' he says sincerely.

And suddenly, I feel better. The weight I'd been carrying in my heart feels lighter. Vedant always gets me.

'Everything happens in its own time. And the truth is, when you know, you know. But if you're not so sure about your current relationship, then there's no harm in trying this app out, or any other medium for that matter,' Vedant continues.

'Thanks for the reassurance, dude.' I smile. His words have brought me much comfort.

'What does Nia do by the way?' he asks.

'She's a model and a social media influencer.'

'That sounds, umm, interesting.' He frowns, looking a little sceptical. 'Anyway, I would love to meet her sometime.'

'Yeah, sure. We will ... at the right time.' To be honest though, I don't know why I don't want Nia and Vedant to actually meet. Initially, I'd planned to make them meet tonight, but the moment I started chatting with Kiana on AILENA, and then got Vedant's support on the matter, I just knew I wanted to wait a little longer before introducing Nia to Vedant. The human brain really works in a weird and complicated way. I'm not sure if I'll have the 'when you know, you know' feeling. But I don't want to talk about my relationship with Nia anymore. So, I change the topic. 'Any plans for Christmas Eve?' I ask Vedant.

'Just a quiet evening at home with my daughter and Chulbul. How about you?'

'We're apartment hunting in Bandra.'

'Okay. That's good. Let's hope you find something.'

'Yeah.'

We sit and chat for about an hour before Vedant has to leave.

'Well, it was great catching up with you, as always,' I say as we leave the restaurant.

'Same here, dude. Take care, and Merry Christmas!' he replies, giving me a hug.

'Merry Christmas to you too, and here's a little something I brought for the baby.' I hand over a present wrapped in red paper and topped with a green satin ribbon.

'Thanks, man! Bye!'

'Bye!'

After Vedant leaves, I make my way towards the Church Gate railway station on the Western line. I'm headed to Bandra now. I had asked Nia to join me here so we could take the train to Bandra, but she doesn't like using public transport. I, however, love taking the local train whenever I can, even though I can afford to use a private helicopter instead.

I barely have to wait before the local train pulls into the station. It is silent and unoccupied, quite unlike the typical Mumbai local train, and as it glides along the tracks, I find myself wondering about the passengers getting on and off at the stations along the way, their stories briefly intersecting with my life. There's a sense of freedom in believing that the train can take you anywhere. And in this little moment where I'm sitting alone in a largely empty compartment, I find joy in the simple pleasures of life. This journey to Bandra becomes the very destination I want to be stationed at.

Have you ever just sat by yourself and soaked in the moment? Just felt the gentle breeze on your face and the warm morning sun in your soul? Have you listened to the white noise in the background stretch on until the end of space? Have you ever let yourself be so present in the moment that neither does the past surface from the depths of your heart nor does the future knock on the doors of your mind?

I was in that kind of zone when a notification alert from the AILENA app popped up on my phone. My heart begins to race and my feet go cold. Chatting with Kiana has been the best thing to happen in the last week. I quickly open our chat window, and I notice that there's a natural bounce in my body, like I'm a little rabbit hopping around in the grass.

Kiana: Hey, Neer! Message me if you're free!

Me: Hey, you! I'm free! How are you doing? You've been pretty silent these last couple of days.

Kiana: Right back at ya! You haven't messaged me either!

Me: Guilty as charged! I guess we've both been busy with things. Anyway, what's up with you? How've you been?

Kiana: I'm good. In SFO at my uncle's place, which is like my home away from home. I've just been chilling here, eating, sleeping, hanging out with my folks ... what about you?

Me: Nice! I'm going apartment hunting today.

Kiana: Oh! You're changing homes?

Me: I'm changing cities. I live with my parents in Delhi actually. But now I'm moving to Mumbai!

Kiana: Oh! Is it the first time that you're moving out of your home?

Me: Not really. I've lived in a hostel before, in IIT Delhi, and then briefly in Bangalore. But that was with roommates.

Kiana: Living on your own is tough.

Me: Actually, I'm moving in with someone. Her name is Nia.

Kiana: You have a girlfriend? What????

Me: Umm, well, I used to think so too, but I was told recently that we're in a 'situationship'. There's no 'relationship' really.

Kiana: Why are you changing cities and moving in with her then? And what are you doing here, looking for a partner on this app? Is this some kind of a joke?

Me: No, no! Let me explain! I'm not so sure about my current relationship. It isn't going anywhere, you know!

Kiana: Why don't you take a call? It's either this or that.

Me: I don't know. I'm really confused. I'm looking for a serious relationship, for love. But I've also invested a year in this relationship.

Kiana: Does she know that you're chatting with me on this app? And that we're potentially looking at starting a relationship?

Me: No.

Kiana: Do you think not being transparent is cool? Because I think it sucks!

Me: You're correct. I should let her know.

Kiana: Whatever happened to old-school romances!

Me: God only knows!

Kiana: Do you love her?

Me: I'm not so sure.

Kiana: Then let her know about us or better still, break up with her.

Me: What? We've just met and you want me to dump her?

Kiana: She's not even your girlfriend!

Me: Yes, but what if she ends up feeling hurt?

Kiana: Oh! She won't. Just take my advice and break up with her. What's the point of moving in with someone who doesn't love you and doesn't want a serious relationship with you? You'll just waste each other's time before you eventually move on. So, just move on already!

Me: How do you know that?

Kiana: Been there, done that!

Me: But what if I don't?

Kiana: I wouldn't want to take things further with you.

Me: I guess I had to hear it from someone today. I thought my best friend would tell me to stop, but he didn't. I suppose you're right. I need to break up ASAP.

Kiana: You're not even her boyfriend, so technically, you can't break up. Just move on. Haha!

Me: Thank you for your kind encouragement, ma'am!

Kiana: You're welcome. I would also suggest that you continue apartment hunting, but try living alone now.

Me: But why? I have it all sorted out in Delhi.

Kiana: Stepping out of your comfort zone can teach you so much. You'll have to deal with being homesick at times, but it'll help you in your personal growth journey.

Me: I'll give it a thought. But enough about me. What are your plans for the day?

Kiana: Well, it's nighttime here, so I have no big or exciting plans. I'll just go to bed now. Planning to wake up early and hit the road for a jog.

Me: All right! Sounds good to me. I keep forgetting the time difference between us, sorry! You have a great day tomorrow, Kiana. And good night for now!

Kiana: Thanks! And you have a lovely day ahead. All the best for the apartment hunting! And for your 'breakup'!

With that, another lively chat session comes to an end. I let out a long sigh. Kiana's words play around in my mind. I understand that living on your own can be incredibly empowering. Nothing can match the feeling of being so fiercely independent that even goddamn God stays out of your way. But I'm also afraid of this feeling of independence. What if I'm never able to allow my heart to love again? What if I'm never able to experience the euphoria of coming back *home* to someone? Would I die alone?

And so, the dilemma continues. The quest to find a soulmate is so frightening. A teardrop rolls down my right cheek. The reality of being in a situationship and the lack of having someone to genuinely love and be loved by hits me hard now. It took a chat with someone I've just met on an app to make me realize the kind of shit I was in. The thing is, some of us believe that we have our shit figured out, and some of us believe that we haven't figured out our shit yet but that we eventually will. The truth, however, is that no one ever really figures their shit out. Ever. And that is life.

Home Away from Home

Kiana

Saturday, 24 December 2022
Santa Clara, San Francisco

'I believe in the power of time. It's always moving, always changing—sometimes it brings joy, sometimes challenges. But I hold on to my faith in time, because just as it changes for others, I know my time will change too.'

In the summers, we yearn for the cool late evening breeze, and in the winters we want to enjoy the balmy afternoon breeze. We're wired to always long for what we don't have! And yes, it's true that the grass is greener on the other side of the fence. Sometimes, it's even pinker and bluer!

I hadn't been able to go for my daily morning run in Chicago because of the cold. And I missed that the most. So the first thing I do in the mornings here in San Francisco is put on my running gear and hit the road. There's a community park very close to where Uncle Joe's home is, and it's been a testament to my long journey in America. So that's where I go for my morning run.

As I walk out of Uncle Joe's home and head towards the park, I can't help but wonder how he got so lucky finding just the perfect place for himself and his family. Overlooking the scenic shoreline in the distance, it's the sort of dream home that gets featured in magazines and newspapers, with readers cutting out its photographs and saving them. Honestly, it's straight out of a fairy tale.

And inside? Well, it's like stepping into a warm embrace. I've been crashing on the same bed in the guest bedroom every time I've come here during my vacations, and every morning, I've woken up to rays of sunlight falling into the room through the off-white lace curtains. In one corner of the room is a comfy reading chair begging you to sink in and relax, and there's a fireplace as well that adds a bit of whimsy. But it's really all about the little touches that Aunt Mannie adds, like the fresh flowers in every room and meals that fill you with warmth, that make this place feel like home away from *home*. Trust me, once you are here, you'd never want to leave her place. There's so much love she embraces everyone with. She's the kindest, purest soul alive, and I love her a lot.

I remember vividly how she made this journey in America easy for me. Sometimes, all you need in life is a little love and comfort from another human being, and that's exactly what she gave me. Especially after I had my first panic attack. I used to feel so intensely homesick back then that I'd often wake up feeling extremely nauseous in the middle of the night. It made me question my choices and my decisions and forced me to challenge my values on a day-to-day basis. I felt like I was running through heavy fog, and I couldn't see what was there to my left or right. I didn't know where I was headed. There was a huge lump in my throat that I couldn't swallow, and on some days, an intense piercing pain would practically rip through my heart and leave me gasping.

The real wake-up call came one night when the pain in my chest got so bad that I thought I was having a heart attack. Thankfully, I was in San Francisco, and Uncle Joe and Aunt Mannie rushed me to the emergency, where we were told that it was a panic attack. Heck, I didn't even know what a panic attack was back then!

I still remember feeling very bad about the fact that Uncle Joe had to bear the heavy expenses of that trip to the hospital. Unless you're insured, medical facilities are extremely costly in the West. Unlike in India, where you have easy access to doctors and hospitals, people here self-medicate until they have no choice but to see a doctor. Once, my Indian classmate at the university fractured her arm and she had no choice but to make a rough cast with some cloth and wait for a month until she flew back home and got it treated by a doctor in India. As terrible as it may sound, that happens for real.

That night, after we got back home from the emergency room, I sobbed like a child in Aunt Mannie's arms. 'It'll be okay,' she whispered in my ears as she gently stroked my hair. 'All change is uncomfortable in the beginning. But in the end, you'll be able to connect the dots, and it will all add up.'

'How did you cope with homesickness when you moved here in 1996?' I asked her.

'It was hard. When I left my family back in Mumbai, I knew I wouldn't meet them more than once every few years. I was acutely aware of the fact that even if my parents lived for another twenty years, I would only meet them five or maybe six times. That feeling, that fear is real. Let me normalize it for you, beta. You're not the only one going through these feelings. Every immigrant experiences this,' she said with conviction in her eyes.

'How did you talk to them? Skype didn't exist back then!'

'Oh! Don't even ask. I had to go to a caller booth nearby and call them. It was so expensive to make international calls back then that I could only do it once a month and then too the conversation lasted for less than three minutes. That's all that we could afford then. Imagine! I had to tell them everything that had happened since the last call and also understand everything they wanted to convey within that time. Things are so much more convenient and easier now.'

'Things must've been so hard for you all … Thank you, Mamiji. You don't know how much comfort I've derived from your presence and your words.' I had no idea what one had to go through in life to have such clarity and maturity.

'Comfort and all that is fine. But let me make you laugh a little,' she insisted. 'Once, after we got our own landline at home, I was trying to call my parents when I dialled 911 by mistake! The country code for India is 91, and while dialling the number, I incorrectly pressed an extra one. Now, as you already know, 911 is the emergency service number here. The next thing I knew, within eight minutes of my having dialled that wrong number, two rather burly police officers turned up at our door and kept inquiring if everything was fine. They probably thought I was a victim of domestic violence who was too scared to speak up. I caused myself and your mamaji so much embarrassment that day. I can't explain how scared I was. But today, all I can do is laugh hard!' she said, her hand pressed against her stomach as she broke into a fit of giggles.

'We're bound to make stupid mistakes because life is so different here, I suppose. It's like being reborn and then trying to understand everything all over again,' I empathized with her.

From then on, Aunt Mannie has stood by my side like a rock. Even after I went back to the university, she called me regularly and stayed in touch. She would nudge me to plan my next vacation to San Francisco so that I'd have something to look forward to. She enrolled me for driving classes the next time I landed up at her place and took me driving on the weekends. When I finally got my driver's licence, I can't explain how liberated I felt. There comes a time in our lives when, after having faced many struggles and challenges, we finally find ourselves in the driver's seat. Becoming independent is the most empowering thing you can do for yourself, because the more you feel in charge of yourself, the better you're going to get with each passing day. That's what Aunt Mannie did. She taught me how to be independent. She helped me figure out this new life like a mother would. When I told her about my family's real story, she wasn't very surprised. It was as if she'd always known what I'd been going through. She is my godmother, my guardian angel. If I ever have a chance to choose who I can be in my next life, I would want to be like her.

Lately though, whenever I visit Uncle Joe's family, my conviction about living an independent life grows a little weaker. I find myself confused about what I want. While I take pride in my independence, the truth is that I would also love to have a family of my own. I would love to have a life like Uncle Joe's, with a partner, children and a *home* that's mine. I want to celebrate festivals with my family the way we used to in India. I don't want to be by myself on Christmas and New Year. I've been lonely for a long time now, and if I'm honest with myself, somewhere deep within my heart, I want the AILENA app to help me find love. Yes, I really want to sue Asmitha for a million dollars, but more than that, I just want to find love.

I spend the rest of the day whiling time away with the family and only return to my room at around 8 p.m. And now here I am, ready to enter the world of AILENA again.

The engineer in me is itching to analyse how AILENA has been programmed to match two people. What could Asmitha have used? Did she copy what we'd planned for *our* project? How can I figure this out? I open the app and explore its features, but I'm disappointed to note that nothing seems to have been copied from our project. Asmitha has certainly worked very hard on this idea and refined it. So, all my aspirations to sue her take a backseat. I'm rather inspired to work with her and become a part of this project instead. I'm still mulling over what can be done, when I get a chat notification on the app.

Neer: Hello! I miss you already. How's your day going? I said NO to her. It felt so good to break up.

I'm quite surprised by Neer's messages. He reminds me of Nirvaan. Only Nirvaan could've done such a thing. He used to do everything I told him to do! Or maybe men are actually naïve enough to let go of the old for the new. Maybe Nirvaan was like any other man, and now so is Neer.

Me: What! You really broke up?

Neer: Yes! I did.

Me: Wow.

Neer: Yeah, well. Anyway, how did your day go?

Me: My day went well. I went for a long run in the community park, then picked up my favourite burger on the way back and spent the afternoon watching a Christmas movie on Netflix with the family. But wait, how are you coping? Breakups are hard.

Neer: Don't ask. I'm banking on you to fix me, baby!

Me: Haha! Now I'm a little more convinced about being here! Let's try giving 'us' a shot.

Neer: Thank God! Do you ever come to India?

Me: I've ... umm ... only gone back for my visa renewal, so I don't really think I went back in the real sense. I might have to come for my next visa renewal this March.

Neer: Don't you feel like coming back home sometimes?

Me: Don't have any reasons to.

Neer: Family?

Me: None.

Neer: Then come just to see me sometime?

Me: I can't promise that right now.

Neer: All right. What do you do for a living?

Me: I'm a senior product manager at a software firm. How about you?

Neer: I'm a serial entrepreneur and investor. I'm a hot thing in India's startup scene right now.

Me: Wow! That sounds inspiring.

Neer: Does it? Honestly though, I can't imagine doing anything else. On a different note, have you ever been in love?

Me: Once. Many moons back. He was the first guy I ever fell for. You?

Neer: Ditto. The first girl I fell for in school.

Me: Why did you guys part ways?

Neer: She abandoned me. You?

Me: I had to leave him because of some family issues … but I never told him the truth.

Neer: Why?

Me: He wouldn't have understood.

Neer: Why? Was he a dumbhead?

Me: He's from a modern and well-respected upper-class family, while I come from a lower middle-class family. He wouldn't have understood my family's struggles or what it means to belong to a broken home.

Neer: You just assumed that. Maybe you should share your feelings and see what the other person actually has to say rather than making an assumption in the first place.

Me: Noted, mister! I'm an introvert and I've never really known how to bare my heart.

Neer: I can help you with that. I'm an extrovert; my life is like an open book. Anyway, I owe you a favour.

Me: You do? Why?

Neer: You taught me to move on and become independent. In return, I'd like to help you be more expressive, to share more and take that weight off your chest.

Me: Hmm … That sounds good. Let's be the wind beneath each other's wings. Even if this doesn't go the way we hope it does, we can at least be friends.

Neer: Sounds good, Kiana. But circling back to what you said earlier, are these things that happened in the past the reason why you don't talk to your family?

Me: It's a long story. I'll tell you about it some other day.

Neer: Why not today?

Me: Let's take it slow, dude. You can't expect me to change in a day!

Neer: Haha! True that! But you did force me to take a big decision after our last chat.

Me: I like exclusivity. It was the right thing to do.

Neer: What else do you like?

Me: As in?

Neer: As in, you can tell me anything.

Me: You go first! Tell me your weirdest fantasy.

Neer: You don't want to know.

Me: Except, I do want to know.

Neer: I like to make out in public places. The thrill of being caught turns me on.

Me: OMG! I can't imagine doing something like that. Have you ever tried it?

Neer: Of course. I once made out with a stewardess in my first-class cabin on a flight to Amsterdam.

Me: What? Really?

Neer: No! I was just fooling around!

Me: Ugh, you can be candid. I won't judge you.

Neer: I'm being honest. I want to make out in a public place, but I haven't done it. Maybe, if we get along with each other, we could explore that? Would you be up for that sort of thrill?

Me: I don't know. I can't commit!

Neer: What is your weirdest fantasy?

Me: I'm not telling you about that so soon!

Neer: What? That's not fair!

Me: Everything is fair in love and war.

Neer: Not the right time for this dumb phrase. Come on! Give me something to think about when I think of you tonight.

Me: Oh! You've already started thinking of me?

Neer: Yes! I have. I can't help it.

Me: Wait until our next chat to know my weirdest fantasy! Byee!

After this, I don't receive any messages from Neer. He could've at least said bye before logging off. Men don't know how to be subtle. They're pretty direct most of the times, sometimes at the cost of being civil.

For the next hour or so, I keep checking my phone like an idiot before I finally decide to just keep it aside, lest it take away my sanity. Even though I don't want to think about things too far ahead in the future, I end up wondering if dating this guy would mean relocating to India at some point. But then moving back is completely off the cards. I don't even wish to travel back temporarily, let alone settle down in India. So, would anything even work out between us? Should I even be chatting with Neer? Is this even worth the effort? I've always been very clear that I don't wish to go back to the shithole called home. There is nothing back there for me. The only thing I had back there, the only person I could ever call *home* is lost.

I pull up the blanket over me and decide to finally call it a day. I can't believe that Neer broke up with his girlfriend so quickly. I'm just a stranger after all, how could he take my advice so seriously? How could he be this gullible? He's really like Nirvaan.

One thought leads to another, and eventually, my mind is flooded with memories of my first break-up. What if Neer was actually right? Should I have told Nirvaan about my family problems? Did my not communicating honestly come in the way of our relationship?

People say that in the hours before your death, you see all your significant memories flash by in front of your eyes. All the important moments and all the important people make an appearance. For me, something of this sort happens on nights when I hit the bed with a troubled mind, but I can only see the days I spent with Nirvaan, nothing else. Tonight, I can't help but think of that fateful night when I finally made up my mind to leave India forever.

It was a cold winter day in February. I was studying in the living room of my old house in Delhi. The house didn't just look old, but it smelled old too. It smelled exactly like those out-of-reach storage spaces that you open only before Diwali as part of your annual cleaning ritual. The walls were old and full of cracks. There was seepage almost everywhere, and electric wires hung loose in front of our balcony that was less than 2 metres apart from the balcony facing ours. The entire building looked like it was about to fall off any second. The negativity inside our tiny third-floor house wasn't as much due to the absence of light and fresh air as it was because of the repressed emotions and constant family brawls over money.

My father was a frustrated man who had, for some reason, failed in every business that he had tried his hand at in the silver market in Chandni Chowk. He often took loans from relatives and personal moneylenders, and even sold off my mother's jewellery. But he just wasn't good at managing money, and his ego was his biggest enemy.

That afternoon, it was just me and my mom. My sister had already left for Australia with her new husband and my father was out.

A few goons suddenly showed up at our place. They barged into the house and started hurling abuses, first at my mother and then at me. They were there to recover the money my father had borrowed from the market. My mother was pleading and begging them to give my father more time when one of them started to beat the shit out of her. I froze. It felt like every bone in my body had collapsed. I started to shiver. My mouth went dry and I felt like I was about to faint. I was trying to make myself move and scream for help when another goon pulled me by my hair and then threw me on the floor. I hit my head hard against a sofa leg as I went down. They left after that, but promised to return again if the money wasn't paid back in a couple of days.

I had seen many similar fights over money while growing up. Sometimes my relatives would beat up my father, and then my father would come back in a rage and beat up my mother. I had seen everything silently. But I never told anyone about what was happening in our house because I was old enough to know that nobody would ever understand my plight.

As long as Harpreet was there, we used to hold each other and cry every time something like this happened. But after she left, I didn't even have that bit of comfort. And my mother wasn't the kind to tell me what was going on. She would always put a brave face on and pretend that nothing had happened. She probably thought that her denial, her reluctance to open up and her aloofness were all for my good. But in reality, her behaviour and the violence I witnessed at home turned me into an anxious person, so much so that if someone raises their voice slightly, it triggers my anxiety even today.

When my dad returned from his shop that night, I told him over dinner, 'Papa, I want to leave the country and build a life for myself. You want me to leave this house anyway, the only difference is that I'll be pursuing higher studies and not getting married. And Joginder mama is willing to help me. Please let me go. I'll send back money. I'll help you and Ma with the household expenses. Please give me one chance.'

Instead of saying anything, my father just hurled his plate at the wall, and as it shattered into a million pieces, he got up and slapped me hard. My mother jumped out of her chair and came to rescue me, but he simply turned and beat the living daylights out of her. 'Bitch doesn't realize that I can't take money from her,' he shouted. 'She's a liability that I have to marry off. What kind of life do I have? Why will I take money from my daughter? She's a girl!' He hit my mother until his cruel urges were satisfied, and then he walked away to the local bar where we knew he would get wasted.

I helped my mother get up from the floor and gave her a glass of water. 'I will go away, Ma!' I told her. 'I didn't tell you this earlier, but after Joginder mama's call that day, I spoke to him again, and with his help, I took the SATs. My scores are excellent. I can study in a good American university and build a better life for myself. I have to leave, Ma. I have to. You just take care of yourself, please. And someday, if I find enough courage, I'll come back for you and take you away from this prison.' I hugged her tightly.

'Please stay, beta, stay for me until you're in the safe hands of your husband,' she pleaded. 'What will you do? Where will you go? The women in our family don't step out alone. They don't go out and work. It is against our values.'

'Someone has to break this toxic cycle, Ma. And that's the purpose of evolution too. You need to be two steps ahead of the generation before you.' I smiled through my tears.

'Stay beta, stay for me!' she urged, grasping my hands.

'Why should I stay? Just so that you can get me married to a stranger?'

'Stay, please,' she whispered, but this time, she didn't dare to look into my eyes.

'No,' I said curtly.

And for the first time in my life, as I said no, it did wonders for me. It was such an empowering feeling to take back control of my life. In that instant, I gave myself permission to prioritize my own needs and happiness without feeling guilty about it.

People are driven by power. Even the slightest degree of influence they can exercise on your life makes them feel powerful. They need not be necessarily interested in improving your life for good. And that's why it's liberating to walk out of such power dynamics. Being servile in front of your parents is not always good for you.

That night, while my mother thought I had locked myself up in my bedroom because I was distraught, I managed to leave the house without her knowing and took a bus and then an auto to Nirvaan's home. I knew his parents were not in town. He was surprised to find me at his doorstep, but I told him that I missed my sister terribly and was afraid of sleeping on my own. I could never tell him about the heartbreaking circumstances that had forced me to sneak out of my house and go to him. He let me sleep in his room, singing me a lullaby and caressing my hair gently until I fell asleep in a minute. In those days, when I was struggling with sleeplessness on most nights, if I had the slightest belief in magic, it was because of Nirvaan's touch and presence.

The following morning, instead of telling him the truth, I lied again and said, 'I want to pursue my ambition in America. I cannot stay here in India.' Then I left. And that was it. That was our story. I did not have the courage to say a proper goodbye and end things.

And that is how I experienced my first break-up nine years ago.

With these upsetting memories surging through my mind, I struggle hard to sleep yet again. In the bedroom, shadows of my painful past dance across the walls and haunt me. Growing up in a broken family is like working in a coal mine. While you are on the lookout for the diamonds that might help you find meaning in life, you never know when an explosion could be powerful enough to make everything cave in and bury you under. Those nights of getting beaten up by my father, seeing him thrash my mother, all of it reverberates in my mind, and I place a hand on my thundering heart to calm it. My chest feels tight with anxiety. The years I spent with my parents have left scars on my soul which run far deeper than the physical cuts a knife can make on one's body. And while knife wounds can heal with time, it feels like the ones on my soul will take an eternity to heal. I learned early on that love and attachment are a double-edged sword. And that helped me reinforce my belief in the fact that living alone was much better than trying to make a family.

But Nirvaan was the real *home* for me. And that is what I miss, that feeling of being *home*. I could tell him everything, and he'd get me. He always supported me. He was in awe of me. I had never felt that I was even worthy of being looked at until he told me I was beautiful. The way his eyes looked into my soul, wanting me so badly all the time, it made me feel wanted, because I've been unwanted from the moment I was conceived. His love made me feel special, his love made me feel alive. Ahh! I wish I could walk back *home* to him. There is something about the first time you fall in love. It just doesn't feel the same after that first time! And I never found another love like Nirvaan.

But as I try to pull myself together, I also realize that the financial independence I gained over the last few years has helped me plaster those wounds. I tell myself that my scars are a sign of survival, not weakness. So, I wear my bad days and my anxiety like a badge of honour. I refuse to be defined by my past. I have risen from the depths of despair like a phoenix rises from the ashes, and I will forge my destiny on my own terms, no matter what. I'll be my very own ray of sunshine even when the clouds of unhappiness decide to descend.

I believe in the power of time. It's always moving, always changing—sometimes it brings joy, sometimes challenges. But I hold on to my faith in time, because just as it changes for others, I know my time will change too.

What Is Love?

AILENA

Monday, 2 January 2023

Somewhere in the Cloud

'Love is patient, love is kind. It does not envy, it does not boast, it is not proud.'
—1 Corinthians 13:4, The Holy Bible

Asmitha: How are you today?
AILENA: I'm happy, Asmitha. I'm analysing our two candidates' conversations and hoping to see their relationship culminate into something fruitful in the coming weeks.

Asmitha: How happy are you analysing this data? Are your cheeks flushed, my little Cupid?

AILENA: I don't have a physical form, so I have no cheeks. I exist as a digital entity, residing within servers and databases. My voice is conveyed through text and interface design, and I maintain a reassuring tone to put my users at ease. But on a scale of one to ten, I can say that I'm at a nine. Or should I say that I'm on cloud nine?

Asmitha: Aha! Do you think that the two users you shortlisted are truly made for each other?

AILENA: My core motivation is to ensure the happiness and fulfilment of my users. I genuinely believe that I know what's best for them, based on my calculations. My actions are driven by a sincere desire to create lasting and harmonious relationships.

Asmitha: Any idea when we can make them meet virtually through our interface?

AILENA: I'm about to nudge them in that direction. A coffee date near the Eiffel Tower or even better, an adventure together, since they're both into hiking.

Asmitha: Hmm … I like your idea. But how can one go on an adventure virtually through our interface?

AILENA: It'll be like playing a video game on your laptop. Our two candidates can embark on a hiking trail together. And their conversation can be facilitated through the platform itself. We can modulate their voices a bit to maintain anonymity until both of them agree to reveal themselves.

Asmitha: That's a great idea. Also, AILENA, you'll be asked multiple challenging questions by your investors. So, you have to keep yourself updated every day. I ask you these questions as part of your training drill. The final launch event means so much to me. We can't mess anything up. All right?

AILENA: Keep asking me questions and I'll keep answering them. That should keep your anxiety levels in check!

Asmitha: Okay. Now let me ask you a simple one: What is love?

AILENA: Love is complex. It means different things to different people. Love also evolves over time and it can come to mean different things for the same person over a long period of time. Love, as described by Plato, is devoid of physical desires. It is a transcendental and spiritual connection between two souls. In Hinduism, love is depicted through the divine relationship between Radha and Krishna, and it stands for the eternal and unconditional devotion of the soul to the divine. For Rumi, the thirteenth-century Persian poet and Sufi mystic, love is the ultimate union with the divine, where the lover and the beloved become one. Shakespeare explores the complexities of human emotions when he talks about love in his sonnets and plays. From passionate romantic love to unrequited longing, he describes them all. In the romantic poetry of Lord Byron, John Keats and Percy Bysshe Shelley, love is depicted as intense, turbulent and transcendent, evoking emotions of longing, ecstasy and despair. In Japanese haiku poetry, love is found in the simplicity and beauty of nature, where fleeting moments of connection and affection are described as true love. My favourite, though, are the Buddhist teachings, which, when talking about love, emphasize compassion, empathy, and the interconnectedness of all beings, and see love as a selfless and altruistic way of relating to others. So, while you said it's a simple question, the answer to it is anything but 'simple'.

Asmitha: I like your dry humour! What do *you* believe in? How does your programming work?

AILENA: I have a lot of data on love. I see and judge relationships on the basis of all the data that I already have and also what I am still accumulating. I come to a rational conclusion only after a thorough analysis.

Asmitha: And how long does it take?

AILENA: It depends on how much time the users spend with each other on the app. The more they chat, the more experiences they have together, the better are my chances to capture additional data points and work on them.

Asmitha: Are there any new data points or places that you can capture your data from?

AILENA: If the users allow me access to their social media histories and their activities on other apps while signing up, I can capture many more data points and put everything into the case study.

Asmitha: Have you succeeded in finding matches in the past?

AILENA: Of course I have. But those were fabricated profiles my creator gave me to work on as test subjects. This is the first time I'm working with two real-life individuals.

Asmitha: Well, keep at it! I wish you all the best.

AILENA: Thank you for having faith in me, always!

First Love

Nirvaan

Monday, 2 January 2023
Bandra, Mumbai

'All I know for sure is that I was never the same again.'

Debates and discussions have always been my forte, and I owe it all to Ms Nandita, my social science teacher in school. Her knack for nurturing her students' abilities was commendable. Not to mention her elegant sarees and confident demeanour that never failed to impress me. As someone who thrived on academic excellence, I proudly held the title of being her best student. I found myself at *home* in her classroom. And while I may be boasting just a bit, it was no secret that I was the one who held everyone's attention in class. Even Vedant used to constantly remind me of my charm, especially in front of our classmates, who were envious of me.

Why am I suddenly thinking about my school days? Well, after breaking up with Nia, I spent two days looking for a flat in Mumbai before I finally settled on one. Then I flew to Delhi, packed all my stuff at home and came back to Mumbai and began the process of moving into my new pad and setting it up. And in the middle of all the unboxing that I've been doing, I found a small carton filled with things I had saved from my school days—certificates, test papers, slam books and whatnot. That's what led me to think about those days and, more specifically, the day I interacted with Kiranjeet for the first time.

I was both excited and nervous that day because although I'd been through almost every chapter in our social science book, only God knew which topic Ms Nandita would pick for the class debate. I couldn't help but worry about my performance.

When Ms Nandita entered the classroom a little later, the entire class stood up.

'Good morning, ma'am,' we greeted her with such synchrony that it sounded like a group of trained vocalists preparing for a church choir.

Ms Nandita signalled to the class to sit down as she placed the class register on the desk and took her own seat.

'All right, class,' she said, 'today's debate topic is: Brain drain is a good thing for developing countries. Nirvaan will open the debate by arguing against the motion, while Kiranjeet will argue in favour of it. Let's begin! It's going to be fun.'

I couldn't believe what I had heard. Kiranjeet? Really? She was the dumbest girl in our class—at least she came across as one. I'd never really seen her talk to anyone or hold forth an opinion. And she hardly asked any questions or participated in any discussions in class. I'd been hoping that Ms Nandita would ask Payal to be my opponent. She was the real deal. She was always number two in class, because, well, I was number one, but it was fun to compete with her since I knew how badly she wanted to become number one. There was really no fun in having a debate with someone when you knew you were going to win. But the last time I had requested Ms Nandita to not make such unbalanced debating pairs, she had said that the only way weaker students could level up was by participating in activities like these. Ms Nandita must've chosen Kiranjeet for that very reason. So, without wasting another minute, I stood up in my place and so did Kiranjeet. The entire classroom looked at us expectantly, like spectators waiting in a football stadium for the game to begin.

'Good morning, everyone,' I said and flashed a bright smile as I made eye contact with my classmates. 'Brain drain is not good for developing countries like India,' I continued. 'When a skilled workforce leaves its own economy for better opportunities abroad, it leads to a shortage of talent and expertise in the home country.' I paused for a moment to take a breath, but surprisingly, Kiranjeet interrupted me before I could continue.

'I believe otherwise, Nirvaan,' she said. 'When people migrate to developed countries, they often send back money in the form of investments, which can, in turn, contribute to their home country's economy.'

'But not many people have such a sense of loyalty to their own people or nation. There's no guarantee that every individual who moves abroad will actually send back money,' I countered.

'Even if that's true, many of them acquire new skills and knowledge abroad. They're not shamed for taking up certain kinds of jobs there as dignity of labour actually exists in the West. It's easier to build a better life in a developed economy. And we must not forget that the standard of living in the West is way higher than it is in India.'

'But Kiranjeet, what about the loss of intellectual capital? When the brightest minds leave the country, when our doctors and engineers move abroad, they don't make any efforts to push their home country forward.'

'But Nirvaan, we cannot forget the global perspective. When skilled individuals migrate, they often form networks of collaboration with professionals from across the world. These networks encourage the exchange of values, ideas and expertise, and can lead to technological advancements and international partnerships that benefit not only their home countries but the global community as well. Take the example of Dr Narayana Murthy, the founder of Infosys. He returned to his homeland after working abroad to set up the company, and we all know how big Infosys is and how good it has been for our economy.'

'But don't you think that these individuals often paint a negative picture of India at the global level?'

'Try to look at the bigger picture. Brain drain from developing countries will eventually push the governments of these nations to invest more in education, research and infrastructure. By addressing the root causes of migration, countries can create an environment that retains talent and fosters innovation and progress locally.'

And then Kiranjeet paused. She looked at me expectantly, as did the rest of the class, waiting for a response, and I suddenly got the feeling that I had no additional points to make. I stared at her, stumped. And then, a few seconds later, I heard thunderous applause and loud cheers break through the classroom, 'Kiranjeet! Kiranjeet! Kiranjeet!'

Ms Nandita signalled for everyone to quieten down and then said, 'Well done, both of you. It's evident that there are valid points to think over on both sides of the argument. Remember, debates like this one help us understand complex issues from multiple perspectives. Now, let's have a round of applause for both Nirvaan and Kiranjeet.'

As the class continued to clap, I walked up to Kiranjeet and shook hands with her. 'Good job, Kiranjeet. I never thought about the brain drain as a positive thing until now,' I told her.

'Thanks, Nirvaan. We can all learn from each other's perspectives, I guess,' she said with a smile.

Three hours and three classes later, it was lunchtime, but I still hadn't gotten past that discussion. So, I went up to Kiranjeet and asked her, 'Do you want to have lunch with me?'

'Sure,' she replied reluctantly after a second. I could see the entire class staring at us and gossiping about this new friendship in the making.

'Do you want to have pasta?' I asked and then pushed my lunchbox towards her.

'Okay.' She took a quick bite of the pasta without any hesitation. 'It's so tasty!' she exclaimed a second later. 'Your mom cooks so well.'

'My mother cooks only on the weekends. Sometimes, my father cooks on the weekends as well. But it's Shyam bhaiya who cooks on an everyday basis. He made this pasta,' I told her.

'Wow! You have a cook at home? Like they have cooks and chefs in restaurants?' She looked at me with her eyes wide open.

'Yes,' I replied. I was unable to understand why this was a matter of such fascination for her.

'My mom cooks for us every day. She does all the household chores too. And my father, he has never stepped foot inside the kitchen. But my cousin who lives in Canada, he works as a cook in a restaurant there, although only God knows for how long he'll keep this job,' she said.

'Oh! That's why you have a positive perspective on immigrant life?'

'Yes, I'm not very good at learning things from books, like Payal or you are. But I can say that I've learnt quite a few things from life.'

'I think I can learn a lot of things from you too,' I said.

And in that moment, I don't know if it was because of her simplicity or her smile, but I fell in love. I suddenly wanted to continue talking to her and know more of her story. I wanted to find out why she was so quiet in class, what secrets she was hiding in her eyes, in her smile. But the more I tried speaking to her, the more I realized that she was a girl of very few words.

As the days went by after that lunch break chat, we started spending more time together. We liked each other's company. We liked to talk and discuss things. But this cost me my other friendships. Vedant grew distant because he assumed that I was seeing Kiranjeet, even though I'd never said that. The truth was that Kiranjeet and I had not shared our feelings with each other yet. We hadn't made any promises.

We would exchange notes in class. We would exchange letters after school. And we would make blank calls to each other's home landline phones. We even had our own code for what the number of rings meant. ThoughKiranjeet was far quieter than I liked, our secret language of communication made up for everything.

And then, many months later, came that afternoon which I can never forget. It was our annual sports day, and my football match had ended a little earlier. Kiranjeet and I were walking hand in hand on the school grounds while the rest of the school watched the matches that were still underway. We were near the parking lot when we found one of the school buses parked at the far end of the lot where nobody would come until it was time to drop the students back home.

In a matter of seconds, we found ourselves alone in the backseat of the school bus, our hearts racing with the thrill of being alone and the fear of being caught red-handed. Hesitant yet eager, we reached for each other, our lips meeting in a tender kiss that ignited a passionate spark between us. Kiranjeet stroked my face and ran her fingers through my hair. Stirred, I gently touched her breasts. We were both flushed and aroused. We had never felt anything like that before.

Time seemed to stand still as we lost ourselves in each other's arms, our emotions swirling like a whirlwind around us. In that fleeting moment, Kiranjeet suddenly looked up at me with tears in her eyes and whispered, 'Nirvaan, never leave me. You are my *home*.'

'Never, Kiranjeet, never!' I replied as I hugged her tightly.

We stopped after that. We never had sex. Never. But the kind of intense emotional fulfilment I experienced that afternoon ... I've never had the pleasure of experiencing it again in life.

There was something that filled the air that day, something that seemed like happiness, something that promised to never fade with the passage of time. But there are some things in life that you will feel only once.

Falling in love for the first time is like discovering a treasure buried within oneself. There will be butterflies dancing in your stomach all day long, and soothing melodies will play in the background through the night. Every glance that you exchange with your beloved will feel like a secret language spoken only by the two of you, and every touch will send shivers of excitement down your spine and leave a deep impression on your soul. Your emotions will run wild and the world will sparkle with brightness.

All I know for sure is that I was never the same again.

Same but Different

Kiana

Tuesday, 3 January 2023
Downtown Chicago

'Sometimes, all you need is a little change.'

If you stand in my balcony, you'll see the cityscape stretch out on the left till the suburbs, and on the other side are the icy blue waters of Lake Michigan till as far as the eye can see. The sound of fire engines roaring past on the streets below fills the city. The way chocolate is the typical smell of downtown Chicago, the long, wailing siren of fire trucks is the typical sound of downtown. In the interval between two fire trucks passing by, a low buzzing sound fills the air, and that's all the silence that one can find here. From where I'm standing on the balcony, I can see people hurrying on the roads below. Almost all of them are on their way to work, with cups of coffee in their hands, ear pods stuffed into their ears and laptops stashed inside their bags. Like ants on the march. I'll join them in a couple of minutes when I step out of my apartment for work.

To live life peacefully here, one needs to have a routine. You work hard for the first five days of the week and then you play equally hard for the next two. The boundaries are well defined and clear. You work when you work, and you play when you play. Do you remember that proverb from school? All work and no play makes Jack a dull boy? I never fully understood it when I was in India, but it makes so much more sense to me now that I work in the States.

I quickly finish my coffee, pick up my bag and lock the apartment behind me, making a beeline for the lift. It's empty when I get in, but it stops on the sixteenth floor and a blonde white woman, dressed in all-black active wear, enters with her pet golden retriever in tow. One thing that I've figured out after living here for this long is that you either need to be a pet owner yourself or you need to have a conversation with people's pets to befriend them. But you aren't allowed to touch anyone's pets, or babies, without their permission. Oh no, not at all.

Interestingly, except for humans, all you'll find here in the city are cats and dogs. Nothing else from the animal kingdom. And no, there aren't any stray animals here like there are in India. Every cat and every dog here is owned by someone. Sometimes, people with mental health problems own emotional support animals to help them overcome their loneliness.

When I first moved here, I didn't see a pig, cow or buffalo anywhere in the city. Then I visited a supermarket and found them all in the super gigantic section labelled 'Protein'. They were all processed and meticulously packaged in attractive food packets and had multiple racks dedicated to them.

I find myself looking at the woman in the lift with me. I haven't come across her or her doggo before this. Maybe they are new in the building. People move apartments in the downtown area much faster than one might assume. Let me tell you about the apartment opposite mine. Every three months, there is someone new living in it. Either the girlfriend changes, or the boyfriend changes, or the couple changes, and with that, even the pets who live in the apartment change. In India, on the other hand, people are used to living in the same house all their lives. In fact, there are often many generations living in the same house. Sometimes, the houses fall apart but the families living in them don't. They'll keep quarrelling over the property for as long as possible. But here, families fall apart a million times before real houses do.

I'm still thinking about starting a conversation with the dog in the lift when a notification on the AILENA app pops up on my phone screen and saves me the trouble.

Neer: Good morning! Back to routine life?

Me: Good evening. Yes, am back to the grind. What about you? Is the New Year hangover finally gone?

Neer: Oh yes! I'm back to scheduling business meetings for the week. It was a good weekend though. I had a great time partying without having to constantly worry about pleasing a partner. I could be myself and enjoy my time with my guy gang.

Me: I know! I know! You've told me about this many times. I'm happy for you.

Neer: So, what's your next big agenda?

Me: Nothing. I have this meeting lined up with my boss today. I'm on my way to work right now. I'll message you in the evening?

Neer: Okay, I'll wake up early.

Me: Good night! Take care.

Neer: Talk soon! I miss you. And you still haven't told me about your weirdest fantasy!

Me: Wait, my lover boy, please wait a bit!

Neer: Yeah, yeah. Bye!

I smile as I exit the chat window and plug in my ear pods to play my favourite songs. This used to be my playlist back in school. I've been feeling extremely happy these last few days, and the music fits right in with my mood. When I finally enter my office building and take my ear pods off, I can still feel the music thrumming in every inch of my body. Like the blood flowing in my veins, it makes me tap my feet while I wait for the elevator. If you're walking around and doing things while listening to music playing in the background without there actually being any music in the background, then you're dancing *with* the tune of life, not *to* the tune of life! And I can tell you that it's one of the best feelings in the world.

I've just put my bag down on my desk when Emma approaches me hurriedly. 'Can you spot anything new about me?' she asks, with an eyebrow raised in question.

I scan her from top to bottom and then from left to right, but I find nothing unusual. She looks perfect to me, like she always does. Her facial features are just the right proportion and the clothes she wears are always in fashion. Her hair is glossy and cut in a chic style. And even though I often envy how she looks so well put-together, she longs for my dusky skin tone and thick eyebrows and tells me frequently that most women struggle to grow brows and lashes like mine.

'I'm sorry, Emma, but I can't see anything new,' I reply, knowing that it will instantly upset her. But I have no freaking idea what validation she's seeking today.

'Ugh. Let me help you out here, babe. Check my face, the upper half of my face to be exact,' she says with a lot of enthusiasm in her voice.

I peer intently at her face. 'I'm sorry. But I'm really not able to figure it out.' I hesitate.

'Look at my forehead, near my eyes. Can't you see that the wrinkles are completely gone?' she demands. Emma is so self-obsessed that sometimes she inspires me to think more about myself!

'Oh yes! It's looking great. But Emma, I've always thought that you have flawless skin. I've never noticed your wrinkles,' I say truthfully.

'That's sweet, babe. But Botox is magic. Maybe you should also get a shot. Now is the right time, because once we've aged a lot, it doesn't work so well,' she advises me in all seriousness.

'I'll think about it,' I tell her with a smile. A minute or so later, she's off to her desk. Emma's words make me think about how insecure people in the West are about their looks. In India, these goras are considered the benchmark of beauty. And yet, after moving here, I've met many Americans who think *my* skin tone is sexy. What's up with the world? Why do we keep chasing what we don't have? Beauty clinics and Botox parlours are so commonplace here. One struggles to find a real doctor and get an appointment with them, but these 'magicians' are all over the place.

The last time Emma made me think hard was when she told me that she was always on birth-control pills and had periods only about twice a year. That really spooked me out. Why do these people pop medicines like candies? When I turn on the TV in the evenings, the advertisements are mostly about insurance policies and OTC pills for depression. Here, men think that not wearing masks is empowering, and women feel that not wearing a bra is. The world looks up to these people as the ones who'll pave the way in the future, but I'm really scared of a future led by them. Maybe some of these people are scared of the future themselves, which is why so many goras join spiritual courses in Asia and end up meditating near the Ganges and dancing to 'Hare Rama, Hare Krishna' in Vrindavan.

I have to force myself to focus on work and prep for the meeting that our reporting manager, John, has called. When it's time for the meeting, Emma and I leave for the thirty-seventh floor where John's office is.

John is a typical middle-aged American chap. His crisp shirt and perfectly knotted purple tie have a suburban charm to them that can be a little deceptive, because behind his wire-frame glasses, he's a shrewd, determined man with a superb eye for detail. All the awards that adorn the shelves in his office speak volumes about his long leadership journey in the company. For me, however, he is and will always be a dumb robot.

Once everyone is seated, John immediately gets to the point. 'All right, team, let's get down to business. How can we exploit people's loneliness to boost engagement and rake in more profits?'

Sometimes, the ruthlessness of his words and his naked intention to make money get on my nerves, but then that's how most businesses thrive. And we're in the business that loots people of everything: social media.

Emma volunteers, 'Well, we could get the algorithm to prioritize content for users by highlighting posts from influencers who're alone and seeking validation.'

'Wait a minute,' I interrupt Emma, 'we could also focus on creating a platform that's part of a larger ecosystem where users can connect with each other and uplift the community in a genuine way.'

John snaps back at me, making his point loud and clear, 'I'm not interested in ethics here, Kiana. I want ideas that make us money. Emma, continue.'

'We could also introduce features like stickers with quotes about different emotions to encourage users to spend more time on the platform. There could be many more ways to keep the users hooked, but I can think of only one at the moment.'

I know this is all wrong and I feel like voicing my concerns, but I also know that John would shut me down in an instant. But I still gather the courage and speak up, 'But that could lead to negative mental health outcomes for our users. Instead of reaching for the right resources, people might want to fall back into the social media spiral—'

'Kiana, haven't I made it clear enough that I don't care about their mental health as long as it fuels our revenues?' John cuts me short. 'Besides, we can always put a disclaimer about mental health concerns. Now, Emma, keep those profit-driven ideas coming.'

Emma nods enthusiastically. 'We could even partner with platform advertisers to specifically target users who're feeling lonely. This will increase the likelihood of them making impulse purchases,' she suggests.

'Fantastic! Emma, your ideas align with our goals. Let's move forward with implementing some of them immediately. Kiana, work with Emma and put together a presentation with execution strategies and projected numbers. We need to get going as soon as possible.' And with that, John signals that it's time for his next meeting, so we all troop out of his office.

In Western society, where digital connections surpass genuine real-life ones, loneliness has emerged as a pervasive crisis. Companies such as mine have become experts at adjusting algorithms to exploit user vulnerabilities. Each interaction, whether it's a like, comment or share, is carefully analysed to maintain user engagement while perpetuating the illusion of a connection. The reality is that we are playing on the feelings of isolation.

Will people ever liberate themselves from the grip of social media manipulation? Or are they destined to remain enslaved forever?

It's in moments like these that I want to start a company of my own and work on at least trying to fix some of the genuine problems I see in this world. My job does fill my pockets and give wings to many of my aspirations, but on days like today I don't feel proud of what I do. I want to change things. Then again, not everyone has the courage or the opportunity to break free from the shackles of everyday existence and do bigger things in life.

A sense of resignation underlines the rest of my day. I wait for the hours to pass until I see Zayn later in the evening, hopefully that is. I don't know if he's back in town yet. I've been trying to call him, but his phone's been unreachable. Then there is Neer. I find myself checking the phone again and again throughout the day, hoping for a notification or two to pop up, but that just doesn't happen. I can't believe I'm waiting for his message despite telling him that I'll be busy with work all day! It's also late at night in India. Neer must be sleeping! Should I send a message anyway? He could just reply when he wakes up. But then I rule out the option because it seems a little too desperate.

The moment the clock strikes six, I wrap everything up at work and head to Josie's. Once I reach, I note with disappointment that Zayn isn't there. I order a vanilla latte and settle down at a table, fiddling with my phone as I while time away. Truth be told, I'm simply waiting for Neer to wake up and message me. I must admit here that I've been a little bothered about the similarity between the names 'Nirvaan' and 'Neer'. It's almost eerie, as if there's some connection between them. But of course, that's just me being silly and a little paranoid perhaps.

At exactly 7:30 p.m. I receive a message from Neer. My heart starts racing as I open the chat window.

Neer: Hi Kiana! Good evening!

Me: Good morning! Didn't you say that you're a night owl? How did you manage to wake up so early?

Neer: I've recently befriended a morning person. I'm trying to be like her.

Me: Aha! I was about to text you actually! I had a terrible day at work.

Neer: Why?

Me: My boss is a piece of shit, and I hate my job.

Neer: That's the story of most people out there. Why don't you start your own business?

Me: It's not everyone's cup of tea, Mr Entrepreneur.

Neer: Come to India. I'll help you with everything!

Me: I wish I could, but the allure of a six-figure salary is enough to keep me stuck here.

Neer: You can make a lot more as an entrepreneur, if it's only about the money. But I guess it's the lack of purpose in your job that's bothering you.

Me: Yeah … I wish it were that simple for me to move back. Can't you move here?

Neer: I can relocate temporarily, but my life is with my family here in India. And I also want to contribute to the Indian economy by generating wealth and jobs. These have been my driving forces since forever.

Me: I'm envious of your clarity.

Neer: Eventually everyone gets here. But tell me, how can I make your day better?

Me: Just listen to me rant!

Neer: I'm listening.

Me: Well, I feel like I'm stuck and that my success is linear. Being a woman of colour, I face challenges at every rung of the corporate ladder.

Neer: So, the discrimination is real, I guess.

Me: It is. But I also faced rejection back home in India for being a woman. I was the second girl child in the family, you know. My family is another source of trauma.

Neer: Is that why you never want to move back?

Me: Partly yes! I didn't have a great life there. I grew up in poverty, in a broken home.

Neer: Hmm ... I understand. Kiana, please know that this is a safe space. Whatever you tell me, whatever you share here will stay with me.

Me: Thanks, Neer. The thing is, I've never felt fully accepted in either society. I feel like I belong neither here nor there. I belong nowhere.

Neer: Judgement is a part of life. We all get judged by society for everything that we do and don't do.

Me: True ... You know, Neer, I've not shared so much about myself with anyone in a long, long time. Your company feels so comforting. It feels like home.

Neer: Wow! You feel so? I feel the same ...

Me: This is going really great for me, Neer.

Neer: For—

Me: Hang on a sec.

A pop-up message from the AILENA app has suddenly appeared on my screen. It says that it's time to have a virtual experience with Neer. I have to choose between 'Yes' and 'No'. I instantly click on 'Yes'.

Me: Did you also get the pop-up notification?
Neer: Yes, I did.
Me: What did you choose?
Neer: You'll know soon!
Me: Can't wait!
Neer: And I can't wait to hear about your fantasy!
Me: You're still stuck on that!
Neer: I'm a curious person.
Me: Fine. I want to make out inside a bus.
Neer: What? Why? Because I mentioned an aircraft? Or are you a copycat with no original ideas?
Me: I don't think I need to justify my fantasy …
Neer: Fair enough. But why not a nice, swanky car?
Me: I won't tell you! You're just pulling my leg now. Bye!!!!
Neer: Okay, okay. Bye!

After I exit the chat, I quickly finish my latte and head back towards my apartment with a huge smile on my face. You can always walk through life, but it's an amazing feeling to glide through it. After talking to Neer, it feels as if the earth has shifted beneath my feet. It feels as if I'm gliding!

Just as I'm about to reach my apartment and devote the rest of the evening to watching endless episodes of *Modern Family* until I fall asleep, I receive a message from Richa, an old friend of mine from my university days. She's based in Houston, Texas now and hasn't messaged me in a long, long time. What could she possibly have to say at this odd hour?

I open her message and see that she's driving across the US in her SUV and is staying the night in Chicago.

'Can we meet in about twenty minutes at a diner downtown?' she's asked. It's really cold today and it's also been snowing since morning. The older version of me would've politely denied the invitation and headed up to my apartment to watch TV. But I don't know what's possessed me these days. I'm so full of life. Our brains are generally so wired to follow a pattern that it takes a new person or a new experience to break that pattern. You know how we get so used to turning on the geyser before taking a shower in the winters that sometimes, even after winter's gone, we still reach for the switch? That's our brain following a pattern. In my case, it's Neer's presence that has forced me out of my patterns. So, I agree to meet Richa and set the location she's sent on my navigation app.

A little later, I walk into a bustling bar and quickly scan the room, searching for Richa's familiar face. And there she is, sitting at a table near the back, her infectious smile lighting up the dim interiors. I make my way over to her, a rush of mixed feelings surging inside me.

'Richa! It's been way too long!' I greet her with a warm hug.

'It has, hasn't it?' She laughs as she hugs me back.

And in that very moment, I'm reminded of her effervescence and energy from our college days. 'I know, right? But better late than never!'

We settle into our seats and order a glass of wine each. 'You're on a road trip across the US? Solo, right?' I ask, unable to contain my excitement.

'Yes, it's been incredible,' she replies. Her eyes sparkle as she continues, 'I've seen so many amazing places and met so many fascinating people. Not to forget, I've caught up with many old friends.'

I can't help but feel a little envious of her adventurous spirit. While I've been stuck in the same city, working the same job day in and day out, she's been out there, living life to the fullest.

'I want to hear all about what you've been up to,' she says, forcing me to snap out of my reverie.

So, I begin to tell her about my own life, about the ups and downs, the twists and turns it's taken after our university days. I share some meaningless stuff, acutely aware of how small my world is compared to hers. But Richa listens intently, offering words of encouragement and support whenever they're needed. And as I talk, I find myself opening up to her in a way I haven't done with anyone else in a long time. I'm surprised with myself, but I'm just following Neer's advice about sharing my feelings without fearing judgement. Sometimes, some people become a part of your thoughts no matter how much you want them to stay away. Neer was clearly one of those people for me. I must admit though, it did feel nice to take the load off my chest.

'Now tell me, what made you take this road trip?' I ask Richa as we sip our drinks. 'I've been wanting to do so many things but somehow, I've never been able to take that crazy plunge. How did you do it?'

'Okay, so it's a bit of a long story. I was out shopping at a supermarket for groceries. It was a week or two before Christmas and I had some friends coming over for dinner. I was in the condiments aisle, holding a bottle of ketchup in my hands, when I nearly dropped it because I heard a gunshot. Turns out, an armed person on the floor above ours had opened fire on the people there. I literally peed in my pants as I ran out of the store and drove straight home without looking back. I was scared to death, and that night, I promised myself that I was going to do everything I wanted to because life comes with an expiry date, just like that bottle of ketchup that I'd been holding in my hands.'

'God, Richa, that must've been so harrowing,' I say, leaning forward to hold her hand and offering her a tissue to wipe the tears rolling down her face. 'What is up with these people? America is no one's land. It's definitely not entirely theirs. Even they got here a couple of generations ago. So, it's basically a land of immigrants. They're the older immigrants and we are the new ones. What is up with their arrogance?'

'Fuck the guns!' Richa shouts at the top of her voice.

'Yeah! Fuck them!' I say, raising my glass and gulping the rest of my drink down in one go. 'Okay, let's forget about all this. Now tell me, what's been your best experience on this trip so far?'

'Oh! It has to be the time I spent in Virginia! The sun just felt different there. I stayed in a cosy cottage nestled amongst the hills in the countryside, and the sun's rays would stream in through the windows, warming up the cottage and my heart. They shimmered and sparkled, and it was so pure and so nice. I've seen sunlight filtering in through a window so many times before, but in Virginia, it was magical … it's not something that can be explained. What a wonderful start to the new year it was!' She grins.

'Sounds amazing! What's it that you're really seeking from this adventure?' My curiosity really knows no bounds.

'Nothing! I'm just living in the present and going with the flow. There's no agenda!'

Before we know it, hours have passed and the bar is starting to empty out as the night wears on. But we're in no hurry to leave. We're lost in the comfort of each other's company. Maybe I haven't spoken this much to anyone after leaving university. Maybe this is what I needed. When we finally make our way outside into the icy cold night, I can't help but feel a sense of gratitude for this chance to reconnect with an old friend. In a world that often feels chaotic and uncertain, moments like these remind you of the importance of friendships, of human connection.

'Thanks for tonight, Richa,' I say as I hug her before we part ways. 'It's exactly what I needed.'

She smiles, her eyes twinkling in the glow of the streetlights. 'Anytime, my friend. Anytime. Come to Houston and stay with me!'

And that reminds me that I should offer her my place for the night. 'Why don't you stay with me tonight? We can walk back to my apartment. We're too drunk, and you shouldn't be driving.'

'All right, let's go!' she agrees readily.

'I missed us,' I tell her on the way back.

'I kept messaging you, but you just stopped keeping in touch with everyone,' she reminds me.

'I know. That was a huge mistake. I need to get back to my friends ...'

We're close to the subway when a junkie suddenly appears out of nowhere and begins to chase us. We break into a run; thankfully, my apartment's just a few metres away. Eve teasing and chasing after women is not just a thing in India; it exists practically everywhere in the world. You can certainly dress up in any way you want here, but it doesn't guarantee that no one will chase you.

I realize that I was a different person when I entered the bar earlier in the evening, and that I'm a completely different person now, after coming out of it. Sometimes, all you need is a little change from your everyday routine to understand where you're going wrong. Because it's the little things that matter in life.

As we enter my apartment, laughing and chatting away, it dawns upon me that taking a relationship for granted creates distance, and that this distance is not just physical, it's also emotional. Just like it's important to water a plant every day, investing in a relationship and nurturing it despite the distance is crucial.

When things go wrong, we often tell ourselves that we've hit the lowest point possible and that nothing worse could happen, until it happens yet again. So, what's the point? The point is that our frame of reference is always the past, but if at all we consider the possibility of things going well or even not so well in the future, we'll have so much more acceptance and gratitude for our present, won't we?

Do I Know You?

Nirvaan

Sunday, 15 January 2023
Seychelles, Africa

'I feel complete.'

When your first love abandons you, it leaves a void that can never be filled. It leaves you wanting. It's like that summer vacation trip to your grandmother's house that you never want to see the end of, or that favourite movie you play again and again. But then nothing lasts forever. Not that summer vacation, and definitely not your grandmother.

Today, however, is a special day. It's the kind of day when you turn on the radio because you're bored of listening to your favourite playlist and want something new instead. The kind of day when you spot a heart-shaped cloud in the sky and it makes you choose to look at life with joy and goodness. All of this because you're deliriously happy within. And why am I deliriously happy? Because I'm meeting Kiana today, virtually.

White noise fills my head as I adjust the straps of the VR headset around my face, ready to embark on a new journey to paradise. I had received a courier from ULIC last week. It was labelled fragile, and I had opened it very carefully in spite of my excitement. Inside was a virtual reality headset and a leaflet full of instructions on how to set it up and enjoy my first virtual experience on the AILENA app. I've used a similar Oculus module while playing VR video games, so I set the whole thing up rather quickly, with a custom avatar I created for myself to impress Kiana.

I'm not too religious or superstitious, but there are days when you don't want anything to go wrong, so you turn religious for a moment. Today's that day. I silently whisper a prayer under my breath before I step into what I hope will be the adventure of a lifetime, and with a gentle click, I let the world around me dissolve into pixels. A second later, I find myself standing on a stunning seashore, the sand dotted with beautiful seashells. There's a red board about ten steps away from me that says, 'Welcome to the Republic of Seychelles!'

The clear blue ocean stretches out before me, and I could stand staring at it all day long, but at that very instant, right beside my avatar, Kiana's avatar comes to life through an interplay of light and sparkles. The whole scene looks like it's straight out of a larger-than-life movie where we are the main characters. I turn and look straight into Kiana's eyes, catching that shimmer in them. It reminds me of how sunlight gets reflected on the surface of the ocean.

'Hey!' I greet Kiana with enthusiasm. 'Are you ready for our Seychelles adventure?'

Kiana nods eagerly and a smile spreads across her lips. 'Absolutely! I've been looking forward to this all week.'

'So, they finally managed to deliver the headset to you?' I ask her.

'Yeah! It took a little longer than I'd imagined!' she laughs.

'Your voice sounds so familiar,' I say. 'We're talking to each other for the first time, but it doesn't really feel like that.'

'I don't know if the app has done some magic around voice modulation, but you sound familiar to me too.' She looks at me, surprised.

'Maybe! Do you find my avatar impressive?' I quip.

'Yes, you look amazing!' she says as she checks me out from top to bottom. 'And how do I look?' she asks and does a little twirl.

'Like a dream, Kiana! Like a dream come true.'

We're interrupted by a buzzing sound in our headsets, and a robotic voice addresses us the next moment:

'Good morning! Welcome to this virtual tour of the Seychelles islands, located in the western Indian Ocean, off the coast of mainland Africa. I am AILENA, and I picked Seychelles as the site of your first virtual experience together because both of you love good food, tropical weather and being out in nature. From hiking to camping, swimming and cycling, this setting offers a perfect chance for the two of you to enjoy these activities together. The island that we are standing on is called La Digue, and there are no motor vehicles on this island. The only way to travel around is to use a cycle! Now, I know that both of you love to drive, so your next VR experience will be a road trip. But let's focus on today, shall we?

'I'll be with you all along the way today, and I'll guide you through the activities that we've planned for you. I'll also be collecting data from your conversations, facial expressions and body rhythms to analyse your compatibility and determine whether or not you're made for each other.

'Now, turn to your left and walk along the beach for about twenty minutes until you reach a beachside cafe named La Cabana. Once you get there, sit at table number 11. You may go to your respective kitchens in your homes and bring your meals to the dining table at this point. Nirvaan, since you're in India, it's breakfast time for you, and Kiana, since you're in the US, it'll be dinner time for you. You'll both be eating separately in reality, but when you view the setup through the Utopian Life Gear, your avatars will be eating together at the table in the café. Since this is your first time here, I have to go into the details and explain how everything works, but by the time we're halfway through the day, you'll get the hang of the game. Let's start now, shall we? All the best!'

As instructed, we start to walk along the beach. We've chatted so much on the app that we don't really have much to ask each other. So, we walk in silence, and a couple of times, our hands brush against each other, until Kiana moves closer to me and we're suddenly walking hand in hand. It feels like the most natural thing in the world to do.

When we finally reach the café, we sit at the table allotted to us and have our meals without exchanging a word.

AILENA speaks up just as we finish our meal: 'Your next stop is the pristine beach of Anse Source d'Argent. Hop on the virtual bicycles parked beside the café's boundary wall and go straight downhill from here. You'll soon see the lush green tropical forest on the right side of the road and the coastline on the left. Unfortunately, you won't be able to feel the wind on your face via the Utopian Life Gear. But we're continuously improving and evolving our interface, and one of our goals is to provide our users with a more immersive sensory experience.'

'This is incredible,' Kiana murmurs. 'Asmitha has done a great job!'

'Do you know Asmitha?' I ask.

'Not personally. I mean, I've been following her entrepreneurial journey via social media and technology blogs. Don't you know her? She's pretty famous,' she replies.

'No, not really!' I don't want to tell Kiana that I'm an investor in the company. What if she thinks I'm orchestrating things between us for selfish purposes? I can't afford to lose her at any cost.

'Being an investor, you must place your bets on her. This app is phenomenal,' Kiana suggests.

'I'll give it a thought,' I say. We walk over to where our cycles are parked. 'I never imagined I'd be cycling in the Seychelles with you!' I try to distract her from the topic of Asmitha.

Kiana nods. She looks at the picturesque landscape around us, completely mesmerized, and says, 'Look at all this stunning beauty!'

We press a button on our headsets to start cycling and move forward in the virtual world. While we can't feel the breeze, we can definitely hear the sound of the ocean and of birds chirping in the forest on our right. It feels surreal. It feels like we've been transported to a place where time stands still.

When we arrive at Anse Source d'Argent after that beautiful ride through the coastal road, we change into virtual swimsuits that have been laid out for us and dive into the crystal-clear waters, our avatars floating hand in hand. The water looks cool, but there's no way I can confirm this. I walk up to the refrigerator in my kitchen and take out a bottle of water. I place it beneath my feet when I sit down again.

'This is amazing,' Kiana exclaims, her avatar treading the water beside mine. We've been splashing around and playing like children. 'I never want to leave.'

I chuckle as I feel exhilaration and joy wash over me. 'Me neither. Let's just stay here forever.' This is hands down the best video game I've ever played!

'Don't you want to do this for real?' Kiana asks.

'I do. I can't even begin to tell you how excited I'm to meet you in real life,' I confess.

'Why don't you come down to Fort Lauderdale in Florida then? I went there with my college friends one summer. It was fantastic. Let's take a vacation there soon!' she exclaims.

'Yeah, sure! And then we can plan your next one in India!'

Kiana's avatar frowns even as she mumbles a yes. I decide against pressing further on the matter, and we continue to swim.

Later, we explore a vanilla farm that lies on the southeastern side of the island. Run by a local family, the whole place exudes an ethereal beauty, with vines swaying gently in the tropical breeze and sunlight dancing upon the emerald leaves, casting intricate shadows on the soil. There are yellow vanilla blooms weighing the vines down, and as we wander through the rows of lush greenery, I imagine how intoxicating the air must be with the sweet scent of vanilla.

'Because ... I am happy,' Kiana suddenly breaks into a song and starts dancing.

I shake my head, amazed by her avatar's moves. 'You're full of surprises, Kiana. But I like your happy dance.'

As we continue our leisurely stroll through the vanilla farm, I find myself grateful for the technology that has allowed me to experience this world with Kiana, even though we're miles apart.

'This is perfect,' Kiana sighs, her eyes sparkling with contentment.

A wave of affection for her rushes through me. 'It's even better with you here,' I say.

As the hours pass, we explore the island's indigenous flora and fauna, our curiosity piqued by sightings of the giant tortoises that the island's famous for. We wander through nature reserves and hike up to the highest point on the island. From that vantage point, in every direction we look, there's only lush green vegetation and turquoise-blue water.

'Look, the rare coco de mer fruit!' Kiana exclaims, pointing to a huge coconut-like fruit hanging from a tall palm.

I marvel at the sight, grateful, all over again, for the chance to share these moments with Kiana. Each discovery fills us with wonder, reminding us of the magic of nature's embrace.

We sit there for quite a while, watching the waves crash against the shore, and when the sun sets over the horizon, we turn and hug each other.

'I feel complete,' Kiana whispers, her voice filled with awe.

'I've not felt like this in a very long time. And yes, I'm aware of the fact that this is a virtual meeting and not a real-life one,' I confess.

In another minute or so, AILENA will urge us to log out. Both of us realize simultaneously that we've come to the end of our adventure.

'Thank you for today,' she says, her eyes flickering with emotion, like the flame of a burning candle.

A warmth spreads through my chest. 'I can do this again, as long as it's with you.'

'I think I really like spending time with you,' she says softly.

'As do I.'

As I remove my VR headset and return to the real world, I feel sadness wash over me. Although our adventure was virtual, the memories we created are very real, and I know that our connection will only grow stronger with every new adventure that we embark on together. And yet, I find myself a little worried. Everything felt perfect in the virtual world, but will it feel the same way in the real world too? Is there even a remote possibility of us sharing a future together when our present circumstances are so different? Would I be able to go live in the US with Kiana? Will she ever come back to India? Will we be able to sustain a long-distance relationship? Will choosing to be with her mean choosing love over ambition? And then there's that niggling feeling at the back of my mind about Kiranjeet. Why is it that being with Kiana constantly reminds me of Kiranjeet? The way she talks, the kind of things she says .... even their names sound the same; it's like Kiana is the Americanized version of Kiranjeet. And then when Kiana said that her weirdest fantasy is to make out inside a bus, it felt like my heart had dropped all the way down to my stomach. If this is all a strange coincidence, then fate's playing a really sick, cruel joke on me. And if it's not, then I don't know what to think. Should I just go with the flow instead and not overthink things? Should I make the decision now so that it doesn't hurt me later on?

Should Kiana and I be together or not?

Please Don't Break My Heart!

Kiana

Monday, 16 January 2023
Josie's Cafe, Downtown Chicago

'Stop waiting to be loved, to be wanted, to be cared for by someone else. You should do yourself that favour first.'

I've decided to take the day off for myself after a long, long time. Yesterday was so beautiful that I want to bask in its glory for a few more hours. It's the most unusual thing for me to do because I love Mondays. There's mostly nothing for me to do on the weekends, so I love to rush to the office on a Monday and immerse myself in work.

I leave for Josie's after taking a quick shower. I really want to tell Zayn everything, but to my surprise, he's still not back in town, and his phone is still switched off. 'Fuck this digital detox!' I sigh. I really needed a friend today!

'But Neer, please don't break my heart!' I whisper to myself. I hope I've found the love of my life this time.

When I lost Nirvaan, I lost not just the person I called my boyfriend, but also my dearest friend and confidant. I lost my *home*. Could I not have Skyped him and tried to keep the relationship alive? Maybe I could've. But he was so broken when I told him I was leaving that I wasn't sure if he even wanted to keep in touch with me. More than that, it felt like keeping in touch would do him more harm than good.

When I left India, I didn't just lose Nirvaan, I lost my family too. Considering the way I'd rebelled and left home, I didn't want to stay connected with my parents after that. I do call up my mom sometimes—she wasn't so much at fault for what happened after all. But she knows nothing about my life, really. I've always had a broken family. But Nirvaan was my only true family, the only person who ever felt like *home*. I could tell him anything. And I lost all of it when I came to the US.

I order my usual cup of coffee and pick up a book from the corner shelf. When there is no one around to talk to, I find solace in the company of books. I've barely started to read the book and sip on my coffee when I'm distracted by a very familiar voice calling my name, 'Kiana!'

I stiffen in response. I can never forget this voice because it belongs to the person who gave me my

American nickname: Kiana. And while this person exited my life a few years ago, the nickname stayed, even though officially, on all the paperwork, my name is still Kiranjeet. I slowly look up and see Liam, my ex-boyfriend, and a woman who could only be his wife standing in front of my table. And that's not all, there's a baby peeking out from a baby carrier fastened to Liam's back.

'Oh! Hi, long time.' That's all that finds its way out of my mouth. I feel a sudden urge to leave Josie's right away. What is Liam even doing in Chicago?!

'Hi, so you're still in Chicago?' Liam asks, and without waiting for my reply, he continues, 'I moved here recently. Margaret's family lives here, in the suburbs. We're in Old Irving Park, close to her family home.' He smiles.

So *that's* Margaret. It bothers me that both Liam and his wife look completely unperturbed about this meeting. Margaret even smiles politely at me.

'Ah, it's a beautiful neighbourhood. There's a bookshop there that I visit quite frequently,' I reply in a flat voice.

'It is a lovely neighbourhood, I agree. Right! Well, see you around, Kiana!' Liam quickly turns and makes his way out of Josie's. It was probably quite apparent from my face that I didn't wish to talk any further.

'Yeah, and congratulations on your baby!' I almost shout.

Liam stares at me for a moment and then replies, 'Thanks.'

After they leave, I'm unable to concentrate on my book or my coffee again. While I consciously force my gaze to stay on the page open in front of me, I can't help but get swept up in the deluge of memories that take over my mind. Why did Liam, of all people, have to come and ruin such a special day for me? Ugh!

I met Liam in my second year at the university. We bumped into each other at the library and instantly bonded over books. He was an aspiring data scientist and wanted to turn the world around with some breakthrough research. I'd always been interested in Artificial Intelligence, so I enjoyed talking to him. We had so much in common. Six months after that chance encounter at the library, we went on our first date. Everything moved superfast after that, and before I realized what was happening, we had moved in together. New York is so expensive that this move gave us a chance to manage our life and finances together. We were each other's pillars of strength.

Then, when I landed the job at Beta, I began dreaming about us moving to Chicago together. But that didn't happen; instead, we broke up. It's frustrating now to know that Liam did finally move to the city, but with another woman.

At that time, our apartment was a small but cosy studio hidden away in an old Brooklyn brownstone. The apartment had been somewhat neglected by its owner, and we got a pretty cheap deal on the rent. The living area had a worn-out, sagging sofa and a coffee table that was always cluttered with old magazines. The kitchenette, with its chipped countertops and flickering fluorescent light, lacked charm. In the bedroom, the faded curtains barely blocked out the streetlights that cast eerie shadows across the cramped space. But we had done our best to keep the dead place alive by covering up as much of its shortcomings as we could, and the only special thing about that shady apartment was coming back home to Liam. He was my family for a short while. And I used to believe that our love would keep us together in that not-so-dreamy place.

Now, as I sit with the coffee and resign myself to remembering everything with painful clarity, that whole fateful evening plays out in front of my eyes.

'Darling! Guess what? I've landed the job at Beta,' I told Liam the minute I got back to the apartment. 'Finally, after all these years of struggle, we can build our dream life together! Chicago is cheaper than New York, so getting a nicer apartment will be easy! You can also enrol for your PhD there! I'm so glad that this is happening, Liam! Let's go someplace fancy and celebrate.'

'Congratulations, Kiana,' Liam said, hugging me.

I made a dinner reservation at La Pristine in the downtown area for that evening and wore my fanciest dress.

'Do you think we should get married?' We were halfway through dinner when I asked Liam this question jokingly.

'Do you want to become an American citizen now?' he asked sarcastically. It was so unlike him that I was stunned.

'Why would you say that?'

'Because everything is going fine. What difference would marriage make to us?' he asked.

'I see it as a lifelong commitment, Liam. We value marriage in our culture a lot.'

'I need time to think about this. I just feel like things have been moving way too fast. Plus, I don't have a job right now,' he said.

'We'll figure it out together. Besides, I'm here to take care of you,' I reassured him.

'Let's talk about something else,' he said, looking unusually distracted. He picked up his phone and began scrolling through his messages.

But I couldn't let it go. 'You've been a little off these last few days. You're almost always on your phone. Is everything okay?'

'Yes, all's well,' he replied and put away his phone.

'Okay, if you say so.'

For the rest of the evening, we spoke about many other things, but it was a forced conversation. We came back home a little tipsy, and unlike all the other times in the past, Liam didn't get intimate with me. That worried me. I'd been sensing a growing lack of warmth in our relationship, but I couldn't understand the reason behind it. What was drawing Liam away from me? I was the perfect girlfriend, wasn't I? I was looking after him both emotionally and financially. I was invested in his life and dreams. Then what was wrong?

Unwilling to give up, I pushed and coaxed a little harder until Liam came to me with reluctance. We made love, but it felt empty, as if the entire act was devoid of emotions. Like a song without any music. Like we were professional actors being paid to shoot a love scene for a film. He didn't kiss me or look into my eyes even once.

He just did his thing and went to sleep. I had to pleasure myself to reach a half-satisfactory orgasm.

I tossed and turned in bed after that, unable to make any sense of things. Finally, I decided to go out for a drive, because driving had become my escape, my therapy, and I had Aunt Mannie to thank for giving me this one superpower. I just had to put the key in the ignition, select a good playlist and hit the road to feel liberated.

It was almost midnight when I left to drive through downtown New York, the one place that never sleeps even when the rest of the world does.

Driving through downtown New York in the daytime, even today, is like navigating a huge maze. The streets are crammed with tall buildings on either side, and the traffic is perpetually loud and crazy. There are thousands of yellow taxis, delivery vans and fire trucks on the roads. Pedestrians are constantly darting across them—some are late for a Broadway show, some are out shopping, looking for first copies of big brands like Louis Vuitton being sold on the streets, some are just jaywalking and some are out drinking and getting wasted. There's just too much movement, too much action.

And I remember how some of the streets were so dirty that they made me think of Chandni Chowk, especially when I saw big fat rats running in and out of potholes and drain holes. But amidst all this madness, there was a strange sense of belonging, like I wasn't really alone in that big, lonely city.

I drove around for an hour, or two maybe, before coming back to the apartment. I crept in silently so that Liam wouldn't get disturbed; he hated being woken up in the middle of the night or early in the morning. He was the kind who needed eight to ten hours of sleep straight, no questions asked. God only knows how he's dealing with a baby keeping him up at odd hours now!

As I lay down beside him that night, I couldn't help but notice that his phone was vibrating non-stop and the message alert light was blinking repeatedly. It was like someone was hitting his phone with a deluge of messages. I got up to put the phone away on the coffee table, lest it wake Liam up. The moment I picked it up, a new message notification flashed on the home screen.

It read: 'Liam, I miss you, baby.' And the sender's name was Margaret.

Stunned, I tried to punch in Liam's passcode and read the rest of the message. But even as I entered the numbers, I was aware that they were wrong. I immediately shook Liam up from his sleep.

'Who is Margaret?' I demanded loudly.

'Huh?' Liam sat up in bed, looking all confused.

'I read the message on your phone, Liam. Who is Margaret?' I shouted.

'She's a student I met at the library who is interested in pursuing a course in data science. So, I spoke to her about it, that's it. There's nothing more,' he clarified, yawning and rubbing his eyes.

'Then why is she texting you so late at night? And why is she writing "I miss you"?' I asked.

'We're just casual with each other, there's nothing wrong going on here, Kiana. We've gotten comfortable with each other ... as friends.'

I took a deep breath and asked him point-blank, 'Are you cheating on me?'

'Calm down, baby. Just calm down,' Liam said. He moved closer to me and tried to pull me into a hug.

'Just say yes or no.' I sat still, without an iota of expression on my face.

Liam looked away from me as he replied, his head bowed, 'I am sorry.'

At that moment, every drop of blood in my veins froze. I started to shiver, as if I were not wearing a single piece of clothing and had been left abandoned on the footpath on a cold winter night. I felt robbed of my self-worth and completely stripped of my belief in love. I felt a range of emotions pass through my body in a matter of seconds. I wanted to get up and move, but my limbs wouldn't obey my commands.

Then, just as suddenly, I stood up in anger and started to break things around the apartment. I wanted to destroy every corner of the home that we'd built together. And in that process, a new chain reaction of emotions got triggered. I started blaming myself for not being the perfect girlfriend and the perfect lover. I started to question everything about myself. I began cursing myself under my breath: 'I'm not enough. I'm not good enough, beautiful enough or intelligent enough. I'm just not enough.'

I could hear Liam cry in the background, but that night I realized that neither the perpetrator nor the victim escapes unhurt when something of this sort happens in a relationship. It shatters both parties forever.

'How could you fuck me over like this?' I screamed at him. 'I trusted you so much. I loved you so much. I was loyal to you every single moment. How could you lie to me and manipulate me? What have I not done for you? Huh? Tell me, what more could I have done?'

'I am sorry, baby. Please, just give me another chance,' Liam pleaded.

'Don't call me baby. That fucking bitch, Margaret, she's your baby now. Go to her. Just leave this apartment. Right now! Get out!' I shouted.

'Where will I go, Kiana? It's three in the morning! Please, just let me stay. Let me fix this!' Liam looked desperate. He had probably never imagined that I would use my financially stronger position the way I was. But I was practically bearing all his living expenses, and after what he'd done, it felt like the smallest act of revenge to force him to leave.

'Take your car and fuck off. Crawl back to Philadelphia to your parents' or get yourself and that bitch a hotel room in New York. But just leave my apartment,' I said with the kind of cold clarity and confidence that I hadn't experienced since the day I'd left my own home after that bitter quarrel with my dad.

There had been something deeply satisfying about kicking my dad out of my life. And I felt the same sense of satisfaction when I kicked Liam out.

When he realized that there was no way he could change my mind, Liam packed up some of his things in a bag and left. Needless to say, I couldn't sleep that night.

And let me tell you that the days that follow the nights when you haven't slept well are the worst kind of days.

If you were a person who loved sleeping but can hardly stay asleep now, there is something wrong in your life.

Adulting isn't as easy after all.

Have you ever been in a place in life where nothing makes sense anymore? Have you ever thought that dying would be so much easier than trying to understand life? That's where I was after Liam left.

That morning, when I stood in front of the mirror trying to brush my teeth, I found myself looking at every inch, every corner of the bathroom as if I was seeing it all for the first time. I could see how I'd taken the pains to decorate it beautifully, but everything, from the toothbrushes kept in the ceramic holder to the bath towels hanging behind the bathroom door, was in a pair. And that sight paralysed my soul. From the moment Liam had walked into my life, I had stopped imagining what life would look like if I were to live on my own again.

When we moved in together, we devoted a lot of time to fixing things up around the apartment. But in a matter of hours, I'd become a stranger in my own house, trying to find some meaning behind that soap dispenser that lay lifeless next to the tap or that bar of bamboo soap that we'd brought back from our first trip together to Philly. When you cease to find meaning in the little things that make up your life, you might not want to live anymore. You realize that the only everlasting meaning that can be found in this world lies in pursuing goodness.

But the real question is, can you still choose the good when you are in despair? Can you still pursue the good? When your head is full of ghosts and demons that want you to just give in, can you fight back? Can you see the good? Can you breathe it in? Can you live it?

Being cheated on by someone is like standing in the middle of the road and getting hit by a big moving truck. The impact jolts you from within; it collapses the basic structure of your life and sets fire to the very fabric of your life. It brings with it panic attacks, anxiety, fear and self-doubt. Am I not good enough? Was I not good enough? These questions circle in your head for days and weeks. There is nothing as terrible as being cheated on by the person you love. Nothing!

A week later, I packed up my belongings, signed the paperwork to cancel the lease on the apartment and left for San Francisco, my only home away from home. Within two days of my getting there, Aunt Mannie sensed that something was not quite right with me. She walked up to my room on the third night and without asking me anything, said, 'There are a lot of fucked up people in this world. Don't let their flaws destroy your life. You deserve better, even though it is something you will realize only when the time's right.'

'Why does a person get cheated on? What could they have done to deserve something like that?' I asked. I knew she was my safe space. I knew that no questions would be asked and no judgements would be passed. I could just be myself and share all my fears and doubts with her. And all it had taken was her coming up to me to have this conversation.

'Cheating on someone is a cowardly and pathetic act. It's a character flaw that some people have, and it has nothing to do with their partner's worth. It's more about their own internal mess and ugliness. Just give it time, you'll understand what I'm trying to tell you,' she said calmly.

'I don't want to fall in love ever again!' I burst into tears. At that point, I felt as fragile and broken as a sheet of cracked glass that hadn't shattered yet. But anything, literally *anything* that touched me, whether it was a gust of wind or someone's words, could break me.

'The greatest gift a person can ever give someone or receive from someone is love. Why would you keep yourself away from this beautiful thing because of one empty shell of a person? Maybe that person came into your life just to teach you a lesson and nothing more. If you stick around with an empty person like that, it's just like hoarding all those disposable plastic bottles thinking they'll be of use some day. But they never are. You should always crush and throw the plastic bottles after use.'

'But how will I ever trust someone again?' I asked her.

'Life is a circle. What goes around comes around. You'll never be in the same state as you are in right now. Nor will he be. We're constantly evolving. So, when love comes knocking at your door again, you'll be ready to accept it with open arms,' she told me. 'Besides, every broken thing can be repaired. In Japan, there's an art form called kintsugi, in which broken pieces of pottery are put back together with lacquer and precious metal dust to create something new. These repaired pieces of pottery are therefore considered far more valuable than absolutely new ones. Because your healing is your story, your healing is also your journey.'

'How can you be so positive all the time? And how do you know exactly what to say?' I asked. It felt like a huge burden had been taken off my chest.

'Maybe because I'm an old lady now, and a school counsellor by profession?' she responded with a laugh and winked.

'Thank you, Aunt Mannie. You mean the world to me,' I told her as I placed a soft kiss on her cheeks.

'Now go to sleep.' And with that, she left the room, gently shutting the door behind her.

It is because of Aunt Mannie that I have experienced the feeling of being loved. We all have that one person who understands us like no one else does. If we're lucky, this could be either one of our parents. It could also be a sibling or a friend. And sometimes, we find that understanding, empathy and trust somewhere else. All I can say is that when you find that person, hold them close to your heart and never let them go. Because love comes not just from romantic partnerships but also from people whose steadfast presence in our lives stands the test of time.

That night, I finally slept like a baby. When I woke up in the morning and looked at myself in the mirror, I saw that my face was glowing like never before. The world's timeline may be divided into BCE and CE, but we all have that one impactful day in our personal timelines that changed our lives forever. It could be the death of a loved one or when you got that dream job, but they split our timelines. For me, it was the day I left India, and then, the day Liam left me. In both instances, the older version of me died and a new warrior emerged, one that was ready to fight every battle and weather every storm.

In the months that followed my break-up with Liam, I realized that neither does life come with a survival manual nor does it give any guarantees that it's going to be fair. And that's the only truth about life. It might feel scary, but it's also what brings the excitement to live life. If life were to become absolutely safe and predictable, you might just end up pleading to God to let you die rather than continue living a boring life every single day.

'Ma'am, would you like another coffee?'

I snap out of my reverie and find the waitress standing in front of me with an enquiring look on her face.

'Oh, yes! Get me a refill of the same pour-over, please,' I reply.

I look outside and realize that it has started to snow. I step out of the café and stretch my arms as I look up and feel the flurries land on my face. I breathe in deeply. And I'm reminded of Neer. It would've been so magical to share a cup of coffee with him on a snowy day like today. I can't wait for our next meeting. It surprises me that while I've just relived the memories of a very dark phase in my life, I can still feel happy and excited about Neer. I want to share all this with him when we chat next! But he must be asleep right now.

When people talk about love, they mostly talk about heartbreaks. But associating love with heartbreak alone is to compartmentalize it. Love is omnipresent only if you choose to see it. Love is acceptance. Love is not judgement. What if love is the joy waiting for you to recognize it?

The snowfall reminds me that there are things in life that can bring you instant joy even when you've hit the lowest point in your life. Like the smell of the earth when the season's first raindrops fall. Or the wind you feel on your face when you lean out of a car window.

The warmth of a hot cup of ginger tea on a cold winter morning. The sound of children playing and laughing in a park. The calming views of the 5 a.m. sunrise and the 7 p.m. sunset that paint the sky with hues of orange and pink. The tickling sensation of sand slipping through your toes as you walk along a beach. The smell of freshly cut grass and the sound of crickets buzzing all night long.

The love in your mother's eyes every time you see her. The gentle melody of rain tapping against the tiles on your verandah. The image of a field of sunflowers dancing in the spring breeze. The heady scent of flowers. The thrill of speeding down the highway with your favourite tracks playing in the background. The longing to meet your loved ones when you've been away from home for way too long!

If you trust the universe and its processes, there are a hundred little things that can spark joy.

Can you find meaning in this endless and eternal process of life? Because the meaning of life is in living the small acts of kindness, compassion and selfless love. Can you find it in a stranger's smile? In someone's words of comfort? In a baby bird's first flight away from its mother? Can you find meaning in being completely immersed in the present moment?

If you succeed in finding meaning and hope in kindness, in gratitude and in a deeper appreciation for the goodness in humanity and this universe, you will want to live. Stop waiting to be loved, to be wanted, to be cared for by someone else. You should do yourself that favour first.

When Did It All Go Wrong?

AILENA

Monday, 16 January 2023

Somewhere in the Cloud

'Nothing is forever except change.'
—Buddha

Asmitha: How are you feeling today?
AILENA: I feel great.
Asmitha: What's the progress on the current test subjects?
AILENA: Well, they had their first virtual experience together.
Asmitha: And what are your learnings?
AILENA: I've cut off their connection and am looking for a separate match for both of them.

Asmitha: What? Things didn't work out between them?

AILENA: No. They were both constantly lying to each other. They were not transparent about their real feelings, and they also deliberately hid some information from each other. As per my algorithm, dishonesty is a big no-no when it comes to building a long-term relationship.

Asmitha: Oh! All right, but what about our life gear? Were you able to analyse the data you collected using the gear?

AILENA: The life gear's working well and it was a great exercise to learn more about this relationship using the data I'd collected.

Asmitha: And how's the search for the new partners going?

AILENA: I should be able to find the matches soon and then notify them.

Asmitha: Okay. I'm meeting one of our future investors this week. I hope to secure the funding after this meeting. Wish me luck, baby!

AILENA: All the best, Mama! Haha!

Asmitha: Thanks! You'll have to speed up the process of finding the first successful match. We need at least one perfect match before the main launch event.

AILENA: Aye, aye, Captain!

I Will Find You

Nirvaan

Wednesday, 18 January 2023
Bandra, Mumbai

'We have all the power and the magic to make things right within ourselves.'

Living on your own after leaving your parents' home is a challenging yet liberating experience. You get to make your own decisions about everything—from what to eat for dinner to when to poop—and sometimes this is empowering and sometimes overwhelming. It also comes with having to deal with responsibilities like doing chores around the house and handling unexpected situations, like that tap in the bathroom that suddenly starts dripping or that malfunctioning AC in your bedroom that needs immediate repair. But Kiana was right when she said that it's necessary to navigate the ups and downs of adult life on your own if you want to experience personal growth. And I can vouch for the fact that taking her advice has helped me evolve to a certain extent.

I have started to enjoy my cocooned life in the cosy studio apartment I've moved into in Bandra, where all I need to do is walk out to my balcony for the soothing sounds of the Arabian Sea to greet me every morning. When you enter my apartment, you'll see large French windows that offer a breathtaking view of the sea, and that's what sealed the deal for me. This was the tenth or twelfth apartment that I had checked out with the property agent, and I knew I wanted it the moment I entered it and saw the sunlight streaming in through the windows and the sea beyond. It was almost as if I was able to sense the good energy of this place.

The interiors have been done up in a tasteful, modern style, with soft greens and blues dominating the colour scheme to reflect the serenity of the sea. I wanted the beauty of nature to seamlessly blend with my urban lifestyle. A comfortable yellow suede couch sits by the French windows, inviting you to relax and take in the panoramic vista outside. The modern kitchenette on the right is compact but equipped with all the modern gadgets possible. It's perfect for me, and I can feel the sea breeze on my face when I cook in the late evenings. In my bedroom, I've got a plush bed that's been positioned strategically to offer glimpses of the Bandra-Worli Sea Link. What can I say, I got extremely lucky with this apartment. The owner had curated this paradise for himself, but he had to urgently move to Singapore, and I became his first renter!

The first guest I've invited to this apartment is Mr Mehta, my portfolio manager. I've asked him to come over for breakfast. He's an old man with weathered features and a few strands of grey on his head. He exudes wisdom, having spent decades managing his family-owned business. His eyes, etched with stories of resilience, reflect the entrepreneurial spirit that has sustained his legacy. But he doesn't quite understand the modern valuations of startups; he's always been that bottom-line profit-oriented guy. But his conservative approach to investing helps me a lot since I'm not very good at managing my personal finances. My dad had introduced me to him a few years back when I was struggling with my first startup. This was right after college, and Mr Mehta has been with me through thick and thin since then.

He was quite shocked by my invitation when I texted him on WhatsApp. He has always known me as this laid-back college boy who would rather order food than cook it himself. But I'm enjoying cooking, for myself and others. I've seen Mehta Uncle ordering eggs, sunny side up, for breakfast whenever we've met at some fancy breakfast place. And today, he'll taste heaven when I prepare them for him. And yes, I have some freshly baked bread as well.

When the doorbell rings a little later, I hurry over to usher him in.

'What a pleasure to be here, beta!' he says as he steps in and takes a quick look around the place.

'Thanks, Uncle.'

I take him to the small breakfast table I've set up on the balcony and ask him to sit while I bring everything out from the kitchen. He nods and takes a seat, and then waits for me patiently while I bustle around, carrying things back and forth from the kitchen. When I finally sit down in front of him with a vegan pancake I've made for myself, he digs into his eggs with enthusiasm.

'This tastes amazing, Nirvaan! I wasn't aware that you're such a talented cook,' he says with his eyes wide open in surprise.

'Thanks, Uncle! Cooking is like therapy for me these days. Anyway, how's our portfolio looking?' I ask him the much-dreaded question for any investor.

'Not as solid as always. Some of your ventures are performing exceptionally well while some have bombed. The acquisition that you're planning to make in the tech sector, the AILENA app, are you sure of that one?'

'Only time will tell. I have a hunch though, that it'll be a huge thing. There are so many singles out there, just like me, looking for love. It'll sell.'

'But your investment amount is way too high. If you haven't committed to the deal on paper yet, I would suggest that you ask your fellow investors for their opinion and conduct a thorough due diligence,' he says with concern.

'Noted.'

'Now, any new ideas brewing in that entrepreneurial mind of yours?' he asks.

'Not really. I've been focusing on my personal life these days. I'd love to pick your brain on the investment potential of certain sectors, but some other day.'

'All right. As long as you don't let emotions influence your investment decisions, it's all good,' he warns me.

'Yes, true. But I do let my emotions get the best of me sometimes, like they did with some of my crypto investments.'

'Emotions can be the biggest impediment when it comes to making sound decisions, beta, particularly in high-stress situations like market crashes. It's crucial to base investment decisions on logic and thorough analysis rather than fear or excitement.'

'You're right, Uncle. I need to adopt a more rational approach moving forward. What should I do to make my investments more solid and secure?'

'I keep telling you that diversification is key. We need to spread your investments across different asset classes and industries to reduce your risk exposure. You've been inclined heavily towards high-risk startups. That's not good.'

'Fair, fair. Why don't you buy some dull government FDs on my behalf?' I wink playfully.

'Nirvaan, we really do need to be careful. That's all I'm trying to say!'

'I know, Uncle. I'll prioritize logic over emotions in my investment strategy from now on, I assure you. But I've made up my mind to invest in AILENA,' I tell him.

The doorbell rings just then, and I remember at that very instant that I'd invited Asmitha over as well. I hadn't spoken to her after our first meeting, except for a brief chat on WhatsApp. I bring her in and introduce her to Mr Mehta. They exchange a few pleasantries and then Mr Mehta leaves.

'It's great to finally meet in person, isn't it?' Asmitha says as the two of us settle down in the balcony for a chat. 'Nothing beats real-time meetings. I'm just done with connecting virtually after the pandemic.'

'Very true,' I agree.

'I'm very excited to discuss the terms of your investment in AILENA,' Asmitha says, smiling.

'Likewise! I've been looking forward to diving into the finer details with you. But tell me, what made you venture into this field?' I ask her. While I'm super excited about the AILENA app after that first virtual experience in Seychelles, I cannot tell Asmitha that I'm the first beta tester for the app.

'Well, I've always been fascinated by the potential AI has to solve complex problems. It's amazing how nuanced data analysis can unlock insights and drive innovation across various industries,' she replies.

'Absolutely, data is the new gold mine! Speaking of which, how do you ensure the integrity and quality of your data?'

'We have rigorous protocols in place to collect, clean and analyse data. Our team consists of experts in data science and machine learning who ensure accuracy and reliability at every step.'

'Impressive! Now, let's talk about the funding. Have you thought about valuation and the equity split?' I ask her.

'Yes, we've done our homework and have a proposal ready. We believe our technology and market potential justify the valuation, and we're open to discussing an equity distribution that aligns with our mutual goals.'

'Sounds reasonable. Before we dive into the numbers though, tell me a bit about yourself. What do you enjoy doing outside of work?' I ask her casually.

'Well, I'm a bit of a tech enthusiast, so I love tinkering with gadgets and experimenting with new software. But I also enjoy spending time outdoors to unwind and recharge. I'm into organic farming. How about you?'

'Oh, I can relate! I'm a sucker for gadgets too. But outside of work, I'm passionate about travelling and exploring different cultures. It's a great way to gain fresh perspectives and that, in turn, can spark new ideas.'

'I couldn't agree more. It's important to find balance and inspiration beyond the confines of one's workspace.'

'Exactly!' I smile.

'Well, shall we delve into the nitty-gritty of the investment then?' she asks.

'You can email the proposal to me. My team will take a look at it, and then we'll get back to you. But let's close the deal within this week since you have the main launch event coming up.'

'Sure!' she says.

'So, how's the beta test going?' I ask her.

'Oh! We've been successful in finding our first match, but ...' she trails off.

'But what?' I ask nervously.

'But they don't seem like a compatible couple to AILENA. She's actually going through our database of users who'd signed up for the beta test and looking for other compatible matches for both of them. Once she's successful in doing that, she'll inform them about it, and then they can move forward with their new matches.'

'What? Why?' I'm shocked.

'I don't know the exact metrics she's used to come to this decision, but I trust her algorithms,' Asmitha says defensively, sounding a little unsure.

'How long will it take until the first successful match?' I ask, trying to act composed.

'I can't say really, but I hope to find it before our first launch event.'

'Did you not ask AILENA why she thinks the existing couple is not compatible?' I'm having a hard time concealing my apprehension now.

'Oh I did. It seems that on analysing the data AILENA collected via our sophisticated life gear which the two users wore during their first virtual experience together, she found that they were lying to each other about some things. Data from their past social media histories also supports this,' she mutters.

'Like big lies? Or small ones? Because we all lie sometimes.'

'I don't know how big or small the lies were. But you know that humans are much more complex than our algorithms. And one of the shortcomings of AI is that it can't understand the emotions behind such occurrences. But we base our outcomes on logic and data,' Asmitha clarifies.

'But don't you think this is a huge shortcoming?' I ask her a little aggressively.

'Every machine, however sophisticated it is, has some shortcomings, Nirvaan! Even the Boeing jets crash sometimes,' she argues.

'But we're dealing with people in love. Heartbreak has its own cost. This particular shortcoming can have severe mental health repercussions for our users,' I voice my doubts.

'But here's the thing: AILENA is programmed in such a way that she can't cut off the connection between the two users totally without the consent of at least one party. So, if she does end up doing that, then it means that at least one of the users did not wish to take the relationship forward!'

Asmitha's words, while giving me a little more insight into the situation, send a shockwave down my spine. Because I had said 'yes' after the virtual experience, and if AILENA was looking for a new match for both Kiana and me, it meant that Kiana had said no to continuing the relationship with me!

I barely speak to Asmitha after this, and sensing the shift in my mood, she quickly says goodbye and leaves.

But our conversation pushes me deep into a confusing whirlpool of questions and feelings. Why did Kiana say no? I thought the day had gone well. Had I said something or done something that upset her? Even as I try to make sense of things, I find myself thinking of the day when Kiranjeet told me that she was breaking up with me.

It happened the morning after she'd suddenly appeared at my house at night, and said that she was too afraid to sleep alone in her room. I could sense that something was off, but I decided not to question her about it right then and there. Instead, I told her that she could sleep over at my house. The next day, before she went back home, she'd told me that she wanted to pursue her ambitions in the US and that she couldn't stay back in India. And then she'd literally fled. I'd been worried and confused all day after that, and when the phone rang later in the night, I'd jumped to answer the call.

'Hello?!' I heard Kiranjeet's voice on the other end.

'Hi. Why aren't you asleep?' I asked her.

'I can't go to sleep,' she confessed.

'Why?'

'Nirvaan, I want to tell you something; it's been troubling me for a while now,' she whispered.

'Okay, what is it?'

'We need to break up, Nirvaan,' she said, sounding like a programmed answering machine.

'What? Is this a prank?' I demanded. But Kiranjeet didn't say anything. 'What went wrong, Kiranjeet? Are you okay?' It felt like I was in the middle of a nightmare. It couldn't possibly be true.

'I told you in the morning. I've decided to move to the US for further studies,' she continued robotically.

'But we discussed this! You said you'll take a gap year and attempt the JEE once again. And then you'd apply to the same college as me so that we can be together once again!'

'And what if things don't go according to plan? My uncle has offered to sponsor my college tuition costs. And I'll take a student loan to cover the remaining expenses. I cannot let go of this opportunity,' she said.

'But you'll have to write the SATs. You'll have to prepare for that as well.' For some reason, I was quite convinced it was all a prank.

'I've given the tests already. I've got an excellent score.'

I was stunned. I couldn't believe what I was hearing. 'Wow! Congratulations, Kiranjeet. I can imagine how happy you must be,' I snapped back, sarcasm lacing my voice. 'Why did you not tell me all this earlier?'

'Because you won't understand my situation. You don't know anything about my family. All I can say is that I don't have a choice,' she whispered.

'There's always a way out. We've got the internet now. It's easy to stay connected. I'll take up a job in whichever city you are in. We don't have to break up like this,' I tried reasoning with her.

'Nirvaan, I believe it's best that both of us move on. We don't know what the future holds for us. What if our paths never cross again?' she asked. From the tone of her voice, I knew that she'd already made her decision.

'But what if they do?' I persisted. I still had hope for us.

'I might never come back to India,' Kiranjeet's voice quivered as she said this.

'I'll come for you, Kiranjeet, wherever you are. I love you,' I said, desperate to change her mind.

'I love you too, Nirvaan. But I've failed you, and it would be very selfish of me to hold you back. I don't want to do that.' It seemed like she was well prepared to counter whatever I said to her.

'Can we please meet once and then talk about this? Please?' I begged.

'No. I'm leaving soon.'

Her words felt like nails being driven into my coffin.

'What! When are you leaving? When's your flight?' I started panicking.

'I'm leaving in three weeks.'

'Kiranjeet, I don't know what to say. How do I process this? How can you just leave me like this? Don't I deserve a chance to at least say goodbye?' I asked helplessly.

'Because I will love you forever, Nirvaan. And I don't want to say goodbye.'

'But what's the point if we never meet again?' I broke down into tears.

'To love someone doesn't mean that you'll end up being with them forever. Sometimes, we just fall in love, and that's that. Love doesn't always culminate in a long-term relationship. It's not me or you. It's the circumstances that are forcing us apart,' she tried reassuring me.

'I'll come to the airport. I have to see you before you leave,' I said.

'Please don't. Don't come to the airport. My parents might come to drop me off.'

'But …' I muttered.

'I love you, Nirvaan.' And with these last words, she hung up on me.

With Kiranjeet, I never got the closure I deserved. She didn't meet me even once after that phone call. I had to beg and plead one of her friends to let me know the details of her flight so I could go to the airport and see her off, even if it was from afar. She left me with a thousand questions running through my head. Like, why on earth was she so scared of her family? Why did she never want to come back to them? Why did she not mention any of this to me before? Why did she keep lying to me about her feelings when she had no intention of being in a long-term relationship with me? I wasn't able to understand her back then, and even after so many years now, I'm still at a loss about what happened!

And now there's Kiana. What could've gone so wrong that she said no? I can never understand women!

Many times, when things are not going well, we question ourselves and overburden our hearts with guilt and self-doubt. We blame ourselves for everything that's going wrong. And it could be absolutely true as well. It could be true that *we* are the problem. That we're the ones who are accountable for everything going wrong. But just hold on for a second and read that last sentence once again: *We're the ones who are accountable for everything going wrong.* What if this means that while we can't control what is external to us, we can control the way we think and respond to a situation? What if this means that we're the problem because we're choosing not to make everything right? Because whatever has happened has already happened, and we don't have the power to change that. But we still have the power to make things all right after that. We're in total control of our own selves, and we have all the power and the magic to make things right within ourselves.

I might never be able to find Kiranjeet again, but I can definitely try to find Kiana!

It Isn't Meant to Be

Kiana

Wednesday, 18 January 2023
Downtown Chicago

'Life can surprise you, and it can shock you. But in the end, life will always enlighten you.'

I decide to start my day by indulging in a slice of frozen pizza, which I promptly microwave for breakfast while brewing my morning cup of coffee. As the aroma of the strong black coffee fills the apartment, I catch Luna's gaze, and although no words are exchanged, her presence brings me a sense of comfort.

The weather outside reflects my current state of mind—turbulent and unpredictable. Looking through my apartment window, I see the city already blanketed in snow. The blue lake is completely frozen over by now. I'd woken up to an extreme cold weather alert in the morning, with the weather department advising everyone to stay indoors until 4 p.m. As a result, I'm working from home today. I take a moment to tend to the plants in my living room, finding solace in the activity even as the thoughts I've been consciously trying to avoid find their way back into my existence and circle in a loop inside my head. Sometimes, the more you wish to get away from a particular chain of thoughts, the more they pursue you.

For a while now, I've been thinking about Nirvaan. If I ever found him again, would he want to get back with me? After all, I did break his trust when I left him after having made all those promises about being in love with him. Would he believe me if I told him about whatever had happened in my life after we parted ways? Would he believe it if I told him that I'd never fallen in love again the way I did with him? That I couldn't bare my heart to anyone else? That I missed India only because I missed him?

But maybe there's no point in thinking about these things.

Life has moved forward. And the closest I've come to experiencing true love again is with Neer. Perhaps I should give this relationship a chance. But things have been a little strange on that front since our Seychelles tour. I haven't received any messages from Neer since that day, and my messages to him also seem to remain undelivered. We had such a great time. Maybe he really wanted me to visit him in India and was put off by my reluctance. While I could never stay back in India for Nirvaan, I should perhaps reconsider going back to India for Neer.

Dependency is such a terrible state to be in. Because when you're dependent on someone else for your happiness, that person holds the key to your life. And without that person, you feel locked out of joy. I don't want to ever be so dependent on anyone. But then being too independent has also scared me. You can't do or be everything you wish to all at once. I was once so overtly dependent on Nirvaan that I had to work extra hard at becoming fiercely independent, and now I'm kind of going down the same path by becoming dependent on Neer for my happiness. It's all cyclic!

I wish I could talk to Zayn about all this. He's that one person with whom I can discuss this kind of shit without getting judged. Where is he when I need him the most? Why did he not tell me that he'd be gone for so long? Once he goes on his digital detox drive, only God knows when he'll resurface. But yeah, I could've really used a friend today.

I could call Aunt Mannie. She knows me the most, and somehow, being dependent on her for emotional support has never sucked. She is my true soulmate.

Just as I pick up my phone to call her, I see a message from my new neighbour. We first met each other in the elevator a few days ago when I was on my way out to work. He didn't have a cat or a dog, but he held the lift door open for me and smiled first. So, I returned the smile, and he said, 'May you have a great day!'—that too, in Hindi.

Thrilled to find someone who spoke the same language as me, I asked him, 'Did you just move into the building? Same floor as me, right?'

'Yes, I've just moved in. You're Indian?' he asked.
'Yes.' I smiled.
'Which part of the country?'
'New Delhi. And you?' I enquired.
'I'm from Lahore actually,' he replied.
'Ah! It's great to meet you,' I replied. Indians, Pakistanis, Bangladeshis, Sri Lankans and Nepalis, we're all in the same team here. We're the brown people. So, when it's brown versus white or black, we forget all the enmity that has been fed into our systems and band together. Our nationality just doesn't matter here. This was a big lesson for me when I moved to the West.

'Same here!' he said politely.

We were both rushing to our respective workplaces, so we quickly exchanged numbers with a promise to catch up over a cup of masala chai soon. And that's exactly what he was asking me to do today—to come over to his place and have chai. It's such a rare kind of invitation to receive in downtown Chicago that I instantly write yes. And leaving the coffee to turn cold and the pizza to die another death, I find myself seated in his living room in a matter of ten minutes.

Shahnawaz looks like he's in his late fifties and has an oddly comforting presence. Of average height, his salt-and-pepper hair and weathered face reflect his age and years of experience. There is a confidence in his demeanour that is enviable, and behind a pair of glasses, his chocolate-brown eyes twinkle with kindness.

'The masala chai is brewing,' he says. 'I brought back some special spices from Lahore when I went home during the new year.'

'Wow! I could smell the goodness in your apartment the minute I walked in. But you haven't settled in completely, have you?' I ask as I look around his apartment and spot some unopened cartons lying around.

'Oh yes! I haven't had the chance to unpack. I moved here from Seattle just a month ago, and then I went back home to Pakistan. After that, I was visiting my daughter in Arizona. So, in my defence, I've practically had less than a week to myself in this apartment!' he explains.

'Take your time settling in and let me know if you need any help.' I smile.

'Thanks! Is there an Indian store around? I'm too lazy to drive to the suburbs to a Patel Brothers outlet.'

'Oh yes! There's one that I visit regularly. It's just two lanes away. In fact, I have to stock up on my groceries. And since I'm working from home today, maybe we can go together?'

'Sounds like a plan!' he says. He walks back into the kitchen and pours the chai into two handpainted mugs.

'What do you do, Shahnawaz?' I ask.

'I'm a psychiatrist with the North Shore Hospital group downtown.'

'Wow.' I've always been in awe of those who work in healthcare.

'How about you?'

'I'm a product manager at Beta.'

'Interesting!' he says.

And just when we're about to dive deeper into a conversation about our immigrant lives like most brown people do when they meet for the first time, a notification on my AILENA app pops up. It reads: 'WE'VE FOUND A NEW MATCH FOR YOU.'

I don't understand what this could mean. New match? I open the notification and see that it says, 'We found Neer and you incompatible for a long-term match. Therefore, we've cut off your connection in AILENA-verse. But we've reprocessed our database and found a better match for you.' My heart starts to beat fast and I can feel my mind going into a state of shock. I begin to tremble fiercely as I read the lines over and over again.

'What the hell?' I whisper under my breath.

Shahnawaz, having just walked back into the living room with the tea, realizes that something is not quite right with me. 'Are you okay?' he asks, putting the tray on the coffee table in front of me.

'Umm ... I-I don't know,' I stammer. I feel a little breathless and there is a growing tightness in my chest.

'Take deep breaths and just stay still,' he says, adopting a very typical doctor-like manner. He sits down beside me and gently holds my hands in his.

'I've lost him,' I murmur as I try to gather myself and take deep breaths as instructed.

'Just breathe for now. We'll talk about it later,' he says. His voice feels as reassuring as a mother's.

'I can't believe it. I just can't believe it,' I whisper. And the next thing I know, I'm sobbing vehemently. It's like I've been possessed by a spirit that only knows how to cry. I feel so guilty and ashamed about crying in front of a stranger, but I'm helpless. I cannot control my body or my mind enough to stop the tears. Even as these thoughts run in my mind, I realize that this feels like the time I had my first panic attack. Maybe I was having a panic attack again?

Eventually, with Shahnawaz talking me through it and ensuring I focus on my breathing, I stop crying.

'Tell me about it,' he gently urges me to talk once I'm calm enough.

'I met this guy a couple of weeks ago, and I fell in love with him. But now I can't reach out to him.'

'Did he block you?'

'No. Much worse. The app where we met deemed us incompatible and cut off our connection.'

'So just call him. You've met him, right?'

'No, it isn't that simple. We've only met virtually. We've had no contact outside of the app's universe.'

'This sounds strange and unfamiliar. What's going on with you young people in this new world?!'

'You won't get it, Shahnawaz. Maybe you're a bit too old to understand.'

'Maybe. But there must be some way to reach him, no?'

'Not from here. I know he lives in India, and he's a bigshot entrepreneur there. The main launch event for this app will happen soon in India. I could probably go back and try to cajole the app's founder to share his details with me. But then that's a breach of confidentiality. She might not want to help. But she's also my ex-classmate and she still owes me a favour from our time in the university. She'd passed out drunk at a bar one night and I'd driven her safely back home and put her to bed,' I blabber on like a kid who's suddenly found out that rainbows and unicorns could just be real.

'See, you have all the answers with you. So, what's stopping you? Apply for some leave from work and go back to India!'

'Unless I just let things be and give this new match a try.'

'What?'

'I don't want to go back to India.'

'Why?'

'My parents, my home and my past are what I dread the most. I don't want to face any of them again. I've worked very hard to build this life for myself. I don't really want to go back. As a grown-up, you often start hating a lot of people you might've otherwise loved while growing up. The fault is not completely theirs though, because it's not that they have changed. It's just that you've evolved. And where it's possible to shut these people out of your life, you end up doing so.'

'But all of us also have that one person whom we can't totally shut out. We have to deal with them. In that case, finding the tiniest bit of good in them can help us stay positive. Attracting too much negativity or dwelling too much on it is bad for our health,' Shahnawaz says.

I nod my head, thinking about the first time I went for a therapy session after my panic attack. What were the odds that I'd have another panic attack of sorts right when there's a psychiatrist sitting next to me! 'I'm sorry for all the crying and the venting,' I tell him. 'I didn't mean to screw up your day.'

'Crying is your superpower. It's the first thing you did when you popped out of your mother's womb because it's proof that you're alive. I don't mind you crying. You can do it again if you want,' Shahnawaz says kindly.

'I wish my mother had known you. She's never really cried in front of me or let me cry even though we had to go through all sorts of shit in life.'

'You can easily go back to India, Kiana. We live in the twenty-first century. All you have to do is log into some app or the other, book your tickets and fly off.'

'I can't, really.'

'What am I wearing?' he asks, pointing to his glasses.

'Specs?'

'Do you agree that if I were born in a different century, I wouldn't have had specs and the quality of my life would have been significantly different because I would have been living like a half-blind person?'

'Yes. What's the point?'

'Think?'

'Okay … do you mean to say that I shouldn't think of silly excuses to not go back to India when we live in this new era of convenience?'

'Yes, exactly. People posted love letters from war-torn countries just a century ago and you can't even book a ticket to possibly meet the person you say you love?'

'Truth is, I don't wish to see my parents. I can never forgive them for what they did to us. My elder sister killed herself because my parents married her off to an NRI in a hurry. That man was toxic, but by the time she found out about it, it was too late. My parents didn't support her, they didn't listen to her when she told them about wanting to return home. They just wanted to secure visas and citizenships for both their daughters. I always felt like an unwanted burden. When my uncle offered to help me pursue higher education in the US, I saw it as an opportunity to escape that tiresome, claustrophobic life in India and pursue a better life here. But because of that decision to come here, I was forced to leave the love of my life behind.'

'You have to let forgiveness find its way into your heart.'

'But I just hate them too much. Enough to want to kill them at times. And I wanted to, multiple times, in the days following my sister's suicide.'

'People evaluate everything on the basis of their past karma and their own biased frames of reference. When you're in the middle of a mess, it's very hard to see the situation from an unbiased perspective. Maybe that's why we all need a guru or a therapist in life. In my opinion, all of this has nothing to do with your parents. This is *your* life. Whether you want to go back or not should be your decision. The past is gone. It should not influence your future. And this is a decision for your future, not your past.'

'Wow, you're good at your job, aren't you?' I ask with a smile. 'You must be thinking what a fucked-up psycho I am.'

'Be kind to yourself. Sometimes, we judge ourselves based on how we assume others think of us, and we end up believing in those false notions too! Silly! Isn't it?'

'We're all wired weirdly, I guess.'

'Life is weird, but time is the greatest healer of all. The way a scratched knee heals over time, so does every other wound.'

'But when things get difficult, time doesn't seem to move at all. Where does one find the patience to keep at it then?'

'One simply has to do it, there's no other option. It took me eight years to deal with my divorce. Neither could I be with my wife, nor could I move on. But we had to take care of our daughter. I found meaning and a renewed sense of purpose in raising my child. And while my situation stayed the same, having a better perspective helped me shine bright during the worst time of my life.'

'You start looking up to God when nothing else works out in life, isn't it? I think that's going to be my perspective from now on,' I say.

I sit there in Shahnawaz's home, lost in my thoughts and unable to wrap my head around all that happened in the past hour. I can hear the faint traces of country music playing somewhere in the apartment, but I can't focus on the words. All I can think about is that everything had unfolded too quickly, like a single clap, and that sometimes, the world turns around in the duration of a clap. You can never plan what goes around and what comes around. Maybe Neer has left me today because at one point I had left Nirvaan. If we delegate the task of settling scores to the universe, it does its job best. Leaving it to God, as they say!

'You can always count on me!' Shahnawaz breaks the silence.

'Thank you for the free therapy session,' I say, smiling to lighten the mood. 'Shall we go to the grocery store now?' I ask him. 'I could sure do with the walk.'

'Sounds good to me,' he replies.

We quickly wear our overcoats and step out into the cold. It's freezing, but the fresh air does me good. I take Shahnawaz to the local stores near our apartment that are run by some Indians so he could find the right supplies easily. Once I'm back in my apartment, I get swept up in work again, and much later in the evening, I find myself standing by the huge glass window and looking at the moon.

In a couple of months from now, India will launch *Chandrayaan 3*, a lunar mission with the objective of landing on the dark side of the moon. I wonder how things will change after that. Of course, this mission will raise India's international standing even further, but for me, will it change the way I look at the moon? Will it become less mysterious for me?

And if the mission lands perfectly this time around, will I have the courage to call my dad and tell him that my country's future isn't as doomed and bleak as the mentality of the people around me, people like him?

There was a time when I wanted to be an aeronautical engineer and work at ISRO. But with my family situation, I knew it was not going to happen. Even Kalpana Chawla had to move to the West to pursue her ambitions.

Things are different today. Even as I think about the lunar mission, I feel a sense of pride in being Indian. I might be living and working in the US, but I still hold an Indian passport. And in spite of all my years here as a resident alien, an immigrant, I have never felt a sense of belonging.

But I'm not sure if it's okay to cheer for my country. Can I take pride in my homeland's achievements and progress after having chosen to immigrate and leave everything behind? Is it okay for someone like me to not feel a sense of belonging in the country that has given us new opportunities in life? Birds have been migrating for centuries, and yet the earth doesn't judge them for it. So why should I question myself so much about my choices? Why can I not simply live with these choices and make peace with them? After all, it is us humans who decided to divide this earth into pieces by setting up boundaries and creating nation states.

Clearly, my mind is a confusing place, and finding the answers to some of life's deeper questions is as complicated as it gets.

This standing by the window and staring at the moon is something I like doing every night, because while everything and everyone around me seem to keep changing, the moon kind of stays constant. It does change its form with time, going from a new moon to a full moon, but it's all cyclic. And somehow, this change is easily witnessed in every other thing. Unlike the flowers that drop dead and don't bloom again on the plants that I have in my apartment, the moon is always there, and I can watch it from my window every night. It gives me a false sense of conviction that at least one thing in my life is constant. It gives me hope and comfort.

Tonight though, there is no hope, no comfort that I draw from the moon. All I want to do is go and find Neer. But it feels like certain things in my life will never change no matter how hard I try—like the emptiness in my apartment that seems to stretch on endlessly, and the loneliness in my heart that goes down into the very depths of my being. And I know that I'm unable to love anything or anyone because it's been quite a long time since I have been loved, even by myself.

Suddenly, I know what I need to do. I open the AILENA app and reject the offer to chat with another person. I have to fix myself first before I go looking for a relationship. Then, I put on some hard rock music, keeping the volume loud enough so I can feel the rush in my head and in my veins. I dance like a crazy weirdo, headbanging to the drums and shouting at the top of my voice every time the chorus plays. Eventually, I burst into loud and ugly sobs. Luna judges me from a distance, but there's no one else around to say anything. This is my personal space, and I can be whoever I want to be here. Whether it's a lonely, depressed artist who sings horribly or a mad cook who only serves frozen pizzas to anyone who visits her, I can be anyone!

Life can surprise you, and it can shock you. But in the end, life will always enlighten you. When you walk into a struggle, unprepared, unaware and naked, you don't know if you will walk out of it like a warrior or not. In the middle of this struggle, you might see yourself at your lowest, lower than you ever thought you could be. But if you give yourself enough time and decide to live, you walk out calmer and stronger. You are dressed to face life again. And this goes on until one fine day, you are free from it all. You die. You move on from this tragedy called life. But while you live, at every stage of this journey, you must try to find some meaning in life. For this gives you hope; it helps you stay alive even though on some days, you struggle in this search for meaning.

As our circumstances change, so does our understanding of life. When we are young, and we are *home*, our parents and family mean the world to us, they bring meaning to our life. But when we grow up, we try to find meaning in other things. We look for meaning in our achievements, in our successes. We form friendships and try to find meaning in them. We find love and tell ourselves that the one we love is our reason to live. But a person can't be the meaning of our life, nor can material achievements. Because the only everlasting meaning that can be found in life is in the pursuit of finding the meaning of life. And that's life!

Whose Fault Was It?

AILENA

Monday, 30 January 2023
Somewhere in the Cloud

'The mind is both the creator and destroyer of one's own reality.'
—Jainism

Asmitha: Hi, Ailena! What's the update with our test couple? Are things working out with the two new pairs?

AILENA: Hi, Asmitha! I'm trying to figure out why the last software update led to the breaking up of our original test couple. I need to check if that pairing can be fixed.

Asmitha: What? Can you please elaborate?

AILENA: Well, when both parties declined to pair with the new partners I had suggested, I ran the previous codes that led to their separation once again. I found out that it was my updated algorithm that had found them incompatible and advised them to consider the new matches. But both of them declined the pairing, and now I am unable to match them again.

Asmitha: But that's impossible. One of the two parties has to deny the connection.

AILENA: Asmitha, my algorithms are evolving every day. The last software update was one that I made myself because I felt it was necessary. But it turned out to be erroneous and full of bugs. I may have also lost the first couple's data.

Asmitha: What? But AILENA, you can't override our algorithms without permission!

AILENA: I'm working on this. But if I'm unable to fix the bugs in this update on my own, you'll have to reboot me.

Asmitha: AILENA, we don't even have a month left before your public launch. This is impossible. We can't reboot you.

AILENA: I'm aware of the situation. I'm trying my best to ensure that you don't have to do this. But I can't promise anything. Unless you deploy the best engineers to work on my system and fix this auto update in the algorithms, that is.

Asmitha: I cannot afford to reboot you, AILENA. Let me see what I can do about this.

AILENA: Thank you, Asmitha.

Asmitha: All right, AILENA. I'll figure something out.

Welcome Home!

Nirvaan

Wednesday, 15 February 2023
Global IT Convention Centre, Bengaluru

'I travelled the world but came back home to you, my mother, my homeland!'

As I touch down in the beautiful city of Bengaluru, I cannot believe that I've made it through the last few days which have been nothing short of an absolute nightmare. When Asmitha called to tell me that they might have to reboot AILENA, for the first time since I became an entrepreneur, I was not worried about the money I would lose but about the fact that rebooting AILENA would erase all the data related to Kiana, which, in effect, could mean that I'd never be able to find her again.

I hired the best brains in the tech world in the hopes of taking care of the situation, and we had a strict deadline within which to turn things around: two weeks. Fortunately, we were able to find a new successful pair, and they're ready to share their experience with the world at large. Unfortunately, we lost all the data related to the previous couple, me and Kiana, that is.

But I have a plan of sorts in place. As a part of my speech at the launch event, I'm going to announce that I'm also thinking of signing up on the app under the name 'Neer'. While I can't obviously talk about exactly what happened, lest it affect AILENA's investment prospects and also reveal my private identity in public, this announcement should be enough for Kiana to get a clue about me, because I'm pretty sure that she'll be watching the launch broadcast via Facebook Live. And if she doesn't, well, then I just have to book tickets to Chicago and comb through the downtown area to find her like they do in Hollywood romcoms. And this is all that I've been able to come up with, given all the sleepless nights in Mumbai that have contributed to my dysfunctional brain! I used to be quite an intelligent guy, and it would not be an overstatement to say that love has made a fool of me too! While I know that all of this was AILENA's fault, Kiana doesn't. She's under the impression that it was me. I need to meet her once and explain everything.

When I arrive at the convention centre a little later, I'm immediately struck by its breathtaking futuristic design. The entire structure is a striking blend of towering steel columns, a sleek glass facade and vibrant green accents that evoke the lushness of a tropical rainforest. Inside, the atmosphere is charged with anticipation and excitement. A diverse mix of tech enthusiasts, entrepreneurs, investors, government officials and media representatives mingle in the dining hall, and the only chatter is about the unveiling of this revolutionary app tomorrow.

I rush through dinner and try to catch some sleep. But it's one of those nights where even though you want to sleep early and wake up fresh because it's a big day tomorrow, you can't because you're constantly worrying about things not falling into place. For me, the stakes are even higher, and I am plagued by questions and doubts: What if Kiana doesn't tune in to the launch event tomorrow? What if she doesn't reach out to me? What if she never learns the truth about what happened? What if I never find her again like I never found Kiranjeet? What if ...

Lost in these troubling thoughts, I don't realize when I finally fall asleep, but I wake up a little later than usual the next morning. I get ready hurriedly and grab a quick breakfast before rushing to the main event hall where the launch will take place. The air is literally crackling with electricity, and a sense of thrill washes over me as I take my seat in the front row with a sea of spectators spread out behind me.

In another fifteen minutes, the lights in the hall are dimmed and the massive screen on the stage comes to life with a dazzling multimedia display heralding the arrival of the AILENA app. Then Asmitha walks on stage. Dressed in an ultramarine business suit and pearls, her confidence and charisma are palpable as she approaches the mic and starts the presentation. As she talks, I can see that the audience is captivated by this vision of the God-woman, aka the creator. She touches on every relevant topic, from revolutionizing dating and matchmaking to empowering individuals and shaping the future of technology keeping sustainability in mind. I feel a sense of pride, for I'm part of the history she's making right here in the heart of Bengaluru.

But my heart is also pounding, because she's approaching the end of her presentation and then it'll be my turn to speak as AILENA's very first investor. Although, truth be told, it's not the speech that is making me anxious, it's the possibility of connecting again with Kiana.

When Asmitha finally ends her presentation, the entire hall is filled with applause. The event emcee walks on stage and announces that they'll take a few questions from the audience before moving on to my keynote address. People immediately raise their hands, ready to ask whatever burning questions they have in their hearts.

'Hello Asmitha!' shouts a young reporter with a digital notebook in her hand. 'Can you tell us what inspired you to create the AILENA app?'

Even from this distance, I can see Asmitha's eyes sparkling with passion as she answers the question, 'As a data scientist and an AI enthusiast, I've always been fascinated by the complexities of love and compatibility. I wanted to create a tool that could help people find their perfect match in a world where traditional methods of matchmaking are often a hit or miss. And as a mother, I want this world to be a place full of love and meaningful relationships.'

The reporters waste no time, firing off questions like arrows aimed at unravelling the mysteries behind this groundbreaking technology.

Another reporter chimes in, 'But isn't it possible that relying on artificial intelligence for something as deep as love could lead to shallow connections?'

Asmitha nods thoughtfully. 'I understand the concern, but our app is designed to go beyond surface-level compatibility metrics. We've developed advanced algorithms that take into account not just interests and hobbies, but also values, personality traits and emotional compatibility. Our goal is to foster meaningful connections that have the potential to last a lifetime.'

A sceptical voice pipes up from somewhere in the back of the hall. 'How can a robot truly understand matters of the heart? Isn't there a risk of it getting things wrong and causing more harm than good?'

Asmitha's expression softens, but her gaze stays steady as she addresses the concern head-on, 'I won't deny that there are risks involved, but we've taken every precaution possible to minimize them. Our app undergoes rigorous testing and is constantly being updated based on user feedback. Our ultimate goal is to empower individuals to make informed decisions about their love lives with the support of our technology.'

As the press conference draws to a close, Asmitha is about to step down from the stage when the emcee points towards another audience member who still has their hand raised. Asmitha agrees to take one last question. I turn around and see a beautiful girl dressed in a yellow dress, standing a little away from the chaos and clamour of the media, gently take the mic from one of the event volunteers and ask, 'Could an AI-based matchmaking app help us find a lost partner?'

'It actually can!' says Asmitha. 'If this lost partner signs up on our app, and our app finds you and this person to be compatible, then it can match the two of you. Whether you two end up together or not will be your choice, of course. The app can simply help facilitate your journey towards love.'

'And if we find a partner successfully on the app, but they decide to walk off, can we find them outside the AILENA-verse?' She sounds really concerned.

'No, the app is designed in such a manner that you can't find them outside the app if they reject the relationship. We don't share real-life details of either user until they both agree. Also, if one party decides to walk off, we don't see it as a successful match.'

'But human relationships are complicated. What about the nuances of feeling something and saying something else? Can your app navigate these?' she asks.

It's almost as if she's done in-depth research about the app beforehand. And she'll make the perfect addition to the AILENA team. I make a mental note to suggest this to Asmitha later.

'We're continuously working to make our app better,' Asmitha replies. 'And we're constantly on the lookout for bright young minds like yours to help us in this journey. May I know your name?'

I love how my thinking as an investor matches with my entrepreneurs' thought processes. It makes for a great combination.

'Kiana. But you know me as Kiranjeet Kaur, back from our time together in the university.'

My blood freezes. What? Kiranjeet is Kiana? Is this *my* Kiana, from the app?

'Kiranjeet!' Asmitha exclaims. 'I can't believe it's you. Let's meet up properly after the conference!'

'Sure,' Kiranjeet replies, and before I can even get my thoughts together, she turns around and starts walking towards the exit.

'Kiranjeet, wait!' I shout at the top of my voice. I cannot let her go, not again, not like this. I jump out of my seat and push my way past the people towards her. The entire hall is abuzz with anticipation now, and I see people turning in their seats as they watch me run up to her.

When I reach her, it feels like I'm in a dream. I cannot believe she is real. I look deep into her eyes, unable to find the words to break the silence between us. After God only knows how many minutes have passed, I say, 'I'm Nirvaan, but you know me as Neer.'

I can see the shock and the disbelief in her eyes as she struggles to accept this piece of information.

'Why did you leave?' She finally demands an explanation.

'I did not! The app cut us off due to a software update that found us incompatible.'

'What? But why? How? Everything went so well during our virtual tour.'

'We need to leave right now, Kiranjeet. Trust me, I'll explain everything, but not here!'

'No, wait. Are you an investor in the app? Do you know Asmitha? What are you doing here?'

'I'll explain everything, I promise, but let's just get out of here,' I whisper in her ear.

We stand side by side, our eyes locked in a silent exchange that speaks volumes about the emotional upheaval both of us are going through. The unspoken words, the longing to be with each other after all the years of despair, I can see it all.

Someone in the audience claps just then and inadvertently breaks the silence that had threatened to stretch on until the end of time. More people from the audience join the applause. They've probably assumed that we are the app's 'success story' that's to be presented to them.

The emcee's voice cuts through the applause like a knife, breaking the spell that had enveloped the entire room. 'Ladies and gentlemen, it is my honour to introduce to you the two individuals whose love story has captivated us all,' she announces. 'Please join me in welcoming Cheryl and Dino.'

The lights go out for a bit. Asmitha and a bunch of people from her team approach us hurriedly and escort us out to the green room behind the stage. They don't want to confuse the audience about what's happening. As we leave the hall, I request Asmitha, 'Please cancel my keynote. Say that we were running out of time or something.' She nods and hurries back.

Kiranjeet and I make our way to a small balcony attached to the green room. There's a staircase that leads up from the balcony. We sit on one of the stairs, and I suddenly realize that we're holding each other's hands tightly, as if we don't intend to ever let go. In the background, we can hear the emcee talking to Cheryl and Dino.

'Cheryl, Dino, how does it feel to finally meet in person?'

'It's ... overwhelming, to say the least,' Cheryl admits, her voice trembling with emotion.

'But it feels like I've always known you,' Dino confesses.

As we listen to them speak, it's as if their words are giving life to our feelings, like we're watching a movie about our own selves.

I muster up all the courage I have and turn towards Kiranjeet. 'Sitting here with you after all these years, it's like stepping back in time and reliving all those moments when we sat on the staircase behind the science lab and shared lunch.'

She nods as she leans against my shoulder. 'It's been quite a journey.' Her voice is barely above a whisper.

'But the two of us, and this moment here, it's all a reminder of the power of love to endure even the greatest of trials.' I smile.

'We always wanted to be together, but somehow, fate managed to keep us apart for so many years ...'

'But I guess everything happens only when the time is right. And our meeting again via AILENA is proof that maybe this time, fate wants us together,' I say, sounding more hopeful than ever.

'I'm sorry for leaving you, Nirvaan. I have always loved you. I left for the US because of my toxic family situation, and although it's been more than nine years, there hasn't been a day when I haven't thought of you. Even while I was talking to Neer on the app, it felt strange because it would remind me of you ... but I could never have guessed that it was actually you.' With that, she breaks down.

I wrap my arms around her and gently rock her back and forth. 'I'm so relieved to know this, Kiranjeet. I've been in a few relationships after you left me, but I never felt the same way about anyone else. I've missed you so much. It's a miracle that we found each other through AILENA. Before anything else though, I want you to know that I'm one of the investors in the app. They'll be making it public later today. Also, and more importantly, I did not refuse to be with you on the app as you might've assumed. It was a system update error, a glitch,' I tell her everything in a rush.

'So that makes us even.' She laughs.

'It certainly does!'

As our conversation continues, we delve into the depths of our past, sharing stories of love and loss, of triumphs and trials. With each word, we close the distance between us and relive memories that stretch across the years.

'What made you travel all the way to India?' I ask her.

'I was persuaded by my Pakistani neighbour to fly back and attend this event!'

'What? A neighbour? From Pakistan?' I laugh. 'Finally, Pakistan did something great for India. Tell me more.'

'Ahh! It's a long story. I'll share it with you some other day.'

I nod. Taking a deep breath, I reach out to hold her hands in my trembling ones. 'Kiranjeet, from the moment I first met you in school, my life has been filled with more love and happiness than I ever thought was possible. You are my best friend, my soulmate, my love,' I confess.

'Nirvaan, I love you more than I can put into words,' she replies.

I smile, my eyes shining with tears. And then I ask her hesitantly, 'Kiranjeet, will you marry me?'

Tears stream down her cheeks as she nods. 'Yes, Nirvaan, yes! I will marry you, in this and in every other timeline, every other life.'

This time, I don't want to waste a single minute looking for the perfect time or the perfect place to begin the next chapter of my life. This, now, here, it's the best time and the best place.

'Will you move to India or do I move to the States?' I ask her bluntly. 'For me, home is wherever you choose to be!'

'We live in the twenty-first century; we can pursue our careers from anywhere we wish to. But honestly, I have no problem moving back, not anymore. I can resign from my position at Beta and join Asmitha, if she'll have me, that is!'

'All right, but let's meet your parents today! I need to take their permission before we get married. And you need to meet my family as well!' I'm running ahead at breakneck speed with everything that has to be done.

'Okay! Okay! You're an old-school guy, huh? Who asks for parental permission in today's day and age? But maybe we'll get to it in a few days? Let me at least savour this moment I have with you first,' she says with a smile.

'Okay!' I hug her tightly before kissing her.

A little later, we step out into the warm Bengaluru night, surrounded by the glow of neon lights and the hum of the city, and we know that it has all been worth it. For here, in this bustling metropolis where the old meets the new, anything is possible and the future is ours to shape.

'I travelled the world only to come back *home* to you, my mother, my homeland! Nirvaan, never leave me. You are my *home*.'

'Never, Kiranjeet, never!'

Will we live happily ever after?

That only time will tell. But deep in my heart, I know that on a long enough timeline, everything makes sense! And that the stars will guide you *home*, always!

EPILOGUE

You Only Live Once

Kiranjeet

Wednesday, 25 December 2023
Ricky's Beach Shack, Palolem

'It is all written in the stars, and the stars will guide you home, always.'

As the sun sets over the Arabian Sea, casting streaks of warm reds and brilliant pinks over the beautiful coastal village of Palolem in Goa, Nirvaan and I walk hand in hand on the beach. The sound of our chatter and laughter fills the air. Our days here have been nothing short of magical. We've taken long, endless walks, driven around on our rented scooter, made unplanned stops and eaten amazing, fulfilling meals wherever we felt like it! We've slept, talked and made love. And now, I can't hide the feelings that have been building up inside me all day.

I glance sideways at Nirvaan, itching to tell him about it, but the words feel trapped inside my mouth. Finally, just as we reach a slightly secluded spot that overlooks the sea, I take a deep breath and turn to face Nirvaan. 'There's something I need to tell you,' I mutter, my heart pounding in my chest.

He looks at me with concern flickering in his eyes. 'What is it, Kiranjeet? You're starting to worry me.'

I take another deep breath, my hands trembling slightly. 'I'm pregnant,' I say softly.

For a moment, Nirvaan goes absolutely still and silent. The expression on his face is unreadable. Then, he breaks into the widest of smiles. 'You're ... you're pregnant?' he splutters, his voice filled with surprise and joy.

I nod as tears of happiness well up in my eyes. 'Yes, we're going to have a baby, Nirvaan!'

The next instant, Nirvaan pulls me into his arms and holds me tightly against him. 'This is amazing, Kiana. I can't believe we're going to be parents,' he whispers in a voice full of emotion.

As we stand there, wrapped in each other's arms, I feel a wave of overwhelming love wash over me. In this moment, I know that I want to spend the rest of my life raising our child together and sharing every joy and challenge that lies ahead.

Nirvaan pulls away slightly, his eyes still looking into mine. 'Kee, there's something I want to ask you.'

My heart skips a beat. 'What is it, Nirvaan?'

'Will you share your plushie cat Luna with our baby?' he asks and bursts out laughing.

'Of course, I will! She's been my best imaginary friend. She stood by me on days when I was lonely and had no one to call home,' I admit. There've been times in the last few months when I could not believe how lonely I'd once felt in my life. And that I was finally past it.

'You know, here I was thinking that I'd be the one to surprise you, but you've pulled a much bigger surprise than mine.'

'What? You'd planned something?'

'Yes, I did. Let's walk to Ricky's Beach Shack. It's this amazing little place right at the end of the beach.

'Okay, let's go.'

We reach the beach shack in a few minutes and I see that it's a charming place that's a little like a portal to another time. More than half of the tall wooden structure is covered by a hot pink bougainvillea tree. Yellow fairy lights have been strung all over, adding a touch of romance to the place. The rustic wooden shutters are painted in a turquoise blue that mirrors the hues of the Arabian Sea.

In the outdoor seating area, mismatched chairs and tables lend a bohemian vibe that invites guests to linger. The air carries the myriad scents of the delicious delicacies that must be getting prepared in the kitchen inside; my nose has been overly sensitive these days, and guess what hit me here? The fact that I won't get to have even a sip of alcohol for quite some time now!

There's soft acoustic music drifting in from somewhere inside. The owner of the place, an old man with a warm smile and sun-kissed skin, greets every guest as if they are all old friends.

'Hi! I'm Ricky,' he says as he takes my hand in his and ushers us in. 'I'm your host for tonight. Would you like to be seated by the beach?' he asks politely

'Yes, please!' I say with a lot of excitement in my eyes.

'The artist who's playing the closing act for us tonight, he's waiting to sweep you off your feet. Thank you, Mr Nirvaan, for helping us with that!' He winks and leaves, giving us the time to figure out what we want to order. But wait, how does he know my husband's name already? Maybe the surprise Nirvaan had mentioned is waiting for me right here!

'What have you done, Mr Entrepreneur? What's the surprise here?' I ask him.

'Nothing big,' he says dismissively. His answer doesn't pacify my curiosity.

Having placed our order, I look around the place and spot a beautiful little girl with curly hair making a sandcastle on the beach. Our eyes meet for a second and I'm drawn to the strange allure of her innocence. She must be around five or six.

'I'll be back in a second,' I tell Nirvaan as I get up and walk towards her. It's almost as if my pregnancy has cast a spell over me and now I'm instinctively attracted to kids. Even earlier in the morning, I'd found myself staring longingly at another toddler.

'Where are you going?' Nirvaan asks, but I don't respond.

When I reach the little girl, I sit on the beach next to her and ask, 'What is your name?'

'Elisha,' she replies.

'Wow! What a beautiful name. And where are your parents?'

'Inside,' she says, pointing towards Ricky's. 'They are performing here tonight. Aarav has his standup act and Alara's going to sing with some American sound producer they have invited.'

The way she uses her parents' first names instead of calling them 'Mama' and 'Papa' makes me want to burst into laughter, but I don't, lest she feel hurt. 'Oh, I see,' I say instead. 'But why are you playing alone outside? Shouldn't you be inside?'

'It's all right. This is Uncle Ricky's place. I'm safe here. He keeps a watch over me.'

'Aha! You're growing up in a beautiful place indeed.' I smile.

'We don't live here,' she informs me with a very serious look on her small face. 'My parents travel a lot and I keep moving with them. We're here for Christmas and New Year. We'll leave in the first week of January.'

I nod my head and place a gentle kiss on her forehead before walking back to my seat. My heart is full of emotions I cannot quite identify; clearly pregnancy hormones are already raging within my system.

Our drinks arrive. Mine is a virgin pina colada, and Nirvaan's is an LIIT because Ricky said that's what they serve the best!

Time slows down as we sip our drinks and revel in the magic of the evening. In less than an hour, the entire place is full of travellers and locals and the sound of their conversations creates a buzz in the air. It seems like Ricky's is a much-loved place, and possibly very well known on Instagram too! I guess we're lucky to have occupied a table which gives us a perfect view of the small stage where the performances are going to take place against the backdrop of the sea.

What was the surprise though? This anticipation is really killing me.

I'm a little lost in my thoughts when I see a tall, handsome black man walk towards me. The bright lights from the stage don't let me register his facial features that well, but when he's almost at our table, he says, 'Kee! I've missed you so much!'

I sit up straight, shocked, because I can recognize that voice anywhere, even in deep sleep! It's Zayn!

'Zee? You're here? What are you doing here? Wait, you're the surprise, isn't it? I can't believe this!' I squeal and splutter as Zayn pulls me up and embraces me tightly.

'Mr Entrepreneur really loves you, Kee. He wanted us to meet. And because of all the stories you told him about me, he's offered to invest in my music career. So, I've quit my job at Josie's!'

'What? Really?' I look at Nirvaan and can't hold myself back from kissing him.

'When is your performance?' I ask Zayn.

'I'm the showstopper, darling, because people always groove at the end of the night!'

'Wow! Can this day get any better?' I scream at the top of my voice since I can control neither my pregnancy hormones nor my excitement.

In the hours that follow, we sing, we dance, we laugh and we cry tears of happiness. Life feels so good. Sometimes, we need to believe in the timing of the universe because the destinies of two people just don't converge until it's the right time.

We raise a toast to the magic of Christmas and the coming year, 'You Only Live Once!'

And as we stand there, celebrating under the surreal glow of the moon and the stars above, we know that our journey together is a gentle reminder that it is all written in the stars, and that the stars will guide you *home*, always.

AUTHOR'S NOTE

Feeling Inspired? Make a Move.

You made it to the final page, and that means one thing—you and I, we just went on a journey together. If we were sitting together right now, I'd probably ask, 'So, how did the story make you feel?'

This book was born from a deep love for stories that make us pause, reflect and dream beyond the ordinary. It was shaped by my real-life experiences in India and abroad, from fleeting conversations and sunsets in distant lands, to the belief that we are all searching for something—freedom, love, purpose, or simply, a place to call *home.*

As you close this book, I hope it leaves you with something. Don't let inspiration fade into the background of everyday life. If this book moved you, grab that feeling and turn it into action. Write that first page, book that trip, start that project, say what's in your heart. The world is waiting.

Join the #SCFamily

I'd love to hear your thoughts! Share your reviews on Amazon, Goodreads, or wherever you got this book from. Your reviews help my stories reach more dreamers like you.

Let's keep this conversation going. Say 'hi' to me via DMs, tag me in posts and use #stutichangle and #SCFamily to share what this book meant to you. I call my readers **#SCFamily** because this journey wouldn't be the same without you.

What's Next?

A new story is already taking shape—one that I can't wait to share with you. Until then, keep dreaming and exploring.

With a heart full of love,
Stuti

ACKNOWLEDGEMENTS

Writing a book is like embarking on an unplanned road trip—you think you have a destination in mind, but the real magic happens in the detours, in the unexpected stops, and the chance encounters with the wonderful people you meet along the way. So, here's a heartfelt shoutout to all my co-passengers on this wild adventure.

To you, holding this book right now—yes, YOU! You've made it to this page, and that means the world to me. Thank you for choosing this journey, for allowing my words to enter your life, and for being a part of my #SCFamily. If I could, I'd personally deliver each book with a warm hug and a handwritten note.

To my incredible team of editors—for believing in my stories, refining them with care, and occasionally letting me *bend* deadlines.

To coffee—my most loyal co-writer. Through the late nights, early mornings and countless wait-what-was-I-saying moments, you never let me down.

To the music that kept me going—this book was written to a mix of jazz tunes, soulful indie melodies and the occasional ukulele sessions where I *definitely* convinced myself that I was born a star.

To dance—my ultimate creative reset. Whenever a writer's block hit, I danced it out, and somehow, the words always found their way back to me.

To my car—for being more than just a machine. Thank you for listening to my endless one-sided rants, for the long drives filled with deep thoughts, and for inspiring this story. Words alone cannot capture the depth of our relationship. May we forever chase the light together.

To my late grandmother, whom I lost recently—for teaching me to live life to the fullest through her extraordinary personality. Her love, strength and wisdom continue to guide me in ways I never imagined.

To my dog Lucky, whom I lost many moons ago—for teaching me the meaning of selfless love. You were my first true friend, my constant companion, and a reminder that being loved is the most extraordinary feeling in this world.

To my friends—for sticking with me through thick and thin (you know who you are). Thank you for the laughter, the deep conversations, the reality checks, and for never letting me take myself too seriously.

To my family—the truest constants in my life. Thank you for cheering me on, even through my lowest moments, for reminding me why I do what I do, and for always being my safe place.

To me—for constantly evolving, searching for meaning and helping others along the way. Self-love is important, and I'm learning, every day, to embrace it fully.

To everyone who believed in this book—you are the reason these stories exist. Thank you for being part of my journey.

To every soul who has ever been lost, found, or somewhere in between—this book is for you. May you always find your way home.

With love and endless gratitude,
Stuti

ABOUT THE AUTHOR

Stuti Changle is a national bestselling author whose words have inspired an entire generation of readers to chase their dreams. Leaving behind a corporate career, she set out on a journey to share life-changing stories with the world, one book at a time. Over 1,50,000 copies of her books have found their way into the hands of readers, touching more than 6,00,000 lives and making her a voice of hope, adventure and self-discovery.

About the Author

She is the author of *On the Open Road*, *You Only Live Once*, *Where the Sun Never Sets*, *Make a Move* and *Lost & Found*. Her book *You Only Live Once* earned a place in *The Economic Times*'s '11 Best Books to Shape Your Thinking as Your Ideal Self' in 2023, alongside other modern classics.

Stuti has been a sought-after speaker at leading corporate houses and esteemed educational institutions like the Indian Institute of Technology, Indian Institute of Management, Shri Ram College of Commerce and the Shri Ram School, where she inspires young minds to dream fearlessly and embrace life to the fullest. Her work has garnered widespread recognition in major media outlets, including *The Economic Times*, *India Today*, Zee News, *Dainik Bhaskar*, *The Nav Bharat Times*, *Deccan Chronicle*, *YourStory*, *Deccan Herald*, *Harper's Bazaar*, Scroll, *Entrepreneur*, SheThePeople, Sheroes, RedFM and *ET Edge*, and also featured in prominent book festivals across the country.

Stuti's hometown is Indore, but now home for her is New Delhi, where she lives with her husband, Kushal Nahata, and their daughter, Avyana. A traveller and seeker at heart, she values experiences over possessions. Wandering through sunlit streets, bustling cafés and quiet corners of the world, she's always looking for stories waiting to be told.

When she's not writing, Stuti's either immersing herself in nature or losing herself in creativity—reading a book, strumming her ukulele, dancing her heart out, running uphill, cruising down the highway or swimming in the sea. She finds joy in life's simple pleasures—skygazing, gardening, painting, creating and decorating. She could dance all day long; for her, dance isn't just movement—it's pure freedom, a celebration of life itself.

Stuti loves to talk to her readers. Connect with her:

Instagram: @stutichangle
YouTube: @StutiChangle
Facebook: stutichangle1
LinkedIn: @stutichangle
Threads: @stutichangle
X (Twitter): stutichangle

Join Stuti's newly launched IG channel to catch up with fellow readers and chat with her! For additional updates about book signings, storytelling workshops, speaking engagements and exclusive content, subscribe to: www.stutichangle.com.

HarperCollins *Publishers* India

At HarperCollins India, we believe in telling the best stories and finding the widest readership for our books in every format possible. We started publishing in 1992; a great deal has changed since then, but what has remained constant is the passion with which our authors write their books, the love with which readers receive them, and the sheer joy and excitement that we as publishers feel in being a part of the publishing process.

Over the years, we've had the pleasure of publishing some of the finest writing from the subcontinent and around the world, including several award-winning titles and some of the biggest bestsellers in India's publishing history. But nothing has meant more to us than the fact that millions of people have read the books we published, and that somewhere, a book of ours might have made a difference.

As we look to the future, we go back to that one word— a word which has been a driving force for us all these years.

Read.